THE POISON GARDEN

MISTLETOE

5

JENNIFER ALLIS PROVOST

Contents

Chapter One
Two Kitchens

"We have been driving forever," I whined.

"We have not." Dan didn't take his eyes from the road, which was smart. We were about halfway through our trip to Queens, and this leg involved traveling on a stretch of road in Connecticut that was first constructed almost one hundred years ago. This historically significant highway was extremely narrow, packed with twists and turns, and had a bazillion on ramps, so other cars were constantly being fired at us like the silver orbs in a pinball game.

"We'll be there soon," Dan continued. "Hour, hour and a half, maybe. Two hours, tops."

He reached over and set his hand on my knee, and I did my best to keep my grumbling to myself. The entire reason we were heading to

Queens was so Dan could introduce me to his family. It was also the first time he'd gone home in a few years, so that made this trip extra stressful for both of us.

As if that wasn't enough, this was Christmas week, and Dan's family was all about the holidays. Word on the street was his father might dress up as Santa.

"How long has it been since you went back home for Christmas?" I asked.

"Four years," he replied. "After Charlotte died, it was just too much, what with everyone else getting married and having kids. Don't get me wrong, I was happy for all of them, but I needed to find my own place in the world."

"I get it." My life had quite literally been laid out for me from the day I was born. As the scion of the magically gifted Moore line, my destiny was to become Mistress of Seers. I finally accepted the position a few months ago, but after some time traveling and reality altering situations that escalated from annoying to awful, I walked away from my birthright. That meant no one was leading the seers, but you know what? They're all grownups. They can sort themselves out, and leave me out of their drama.

Now that I'd left wrangling the seers behind, I was figuring out my new life with Dan. He had also recently left his career as a police officer, and we'd gone into business together in my newly reformed private detective agency, Nine Lives Investigations. So far, all of our cases had been boring, and I liked that. We'd already had enough excitement to last us the rest of our lives.

There was also the fact that we were sort of, kind of married, and as far as I knew Dan had yet to share that detail with his parents.

"Have you warned anyone about our handfasting?" I asked. "Or are we just going to walk in wearing matching rings and see how long it takes them to notice?"

"They know."

I did an actual double take. "They do? Since when?"

"I told Alicia," he began, "and she told Ma. Once you tell my mother something everyone knows, and the fastest way to get news to Ma is to tell Alicia."

Alicia was the youngest sibling, and the one Dan talked to the most often, probably because he was the second youngest. Solidarity against the older kids and all. "Have you talked to your parents directly?"

"About us?"

"About anything."

"No."

If he hadn't been driving, I would have smacked him. "Dan. You talk to your mother all the time, but you never mentioned a fricken' serious relationship? What the hell are we walking into?"

"Ma doesn't like to learn things over the phone," he said. "She likes to get news in person. That's why we tell Alicia stuff, so she can deliver it to Ma. And my father doesn't use the phone."

"What? How does he communicate?"

Dan shrugged. "He's old school."

"The telephone was invented in the eighteen seventies, and I'm pretty sure your father was born afterward!"

His gaze slid toward me, then back to the road. "Was yours?"

"Actually, yes." My father was only one hundred and seventeen years old, of which Dan was quite aware. "Seriously, will they be okay with us dropping all of this on them at once?"

"They will be," Dan said. "It really doesn't matter what they've already heard. My parents aren't going to form an opinion about you one way or the other until they meet you in person, and see how you react."

"React to what?"

"Everything."

Almost three hours later, we pulled up in front of Dan's grandmother's house in Queens. It was a split level ranch, and according to Dan, this was where his entire extended family congregated over the holidays. The family was so big the house had two kitchens, one on the first floor where his mother cooked, and one in the basement for his grandmother.

"If it's your gran's house, why does she get stuck cooking in the basement?" I asked, as we got out of the car.

"The downstairs kitchen is the better one," Dan replied. "Nonna holds court down there like an empress. You'll see."

I gazed up at the house. It was nowhere near as old or as big as the place I grew up in, but it was imposing in its own way. "I can't wait."

"Come on, babe." Dan took my hand. "They're gonna love you. Promise."

We left our luggage in the car, since we'd opted for a hotel room instead of staying in the family home. According to Dan, he'd already spent plenty of years fighting his brothers for equal time in the bathroom, and he was ready to move on. As we climbed the front steps, I wondered if Dan finally coming home was almost too much for him to handle, and he'd booked the hotel as a way for him to duck out when he needed to.

Dan opened the front door, and yelled, "Ma, Dad? Nonna? We're here!"

I expected a crowded room packed with unfamiliar faces. Instead, the front room was empty, and the house was dead quiet. "Is anyone home?" I asked.

"Someone's always here," he replied, then we heard footsteps on the stairs. A few moments later, a petite brunette woman burst into the room and leapt into Dan's arms.

"I missed you so much, Danny," the woman said. "You got here just in the nick of time!"

"Nick of time for what?" Dan asked, then he remembered me. "Alicia, this is Eliza. Eli, this is my younger sister."

"Youngest sister," Alicia amended, then she extricated herself from Dan and faced me. She was as pretty as Dan was handsome, and the way she clasped her hands over her heart and grinned told me that at least one of Dan's siblings was glad to meet me. "Eliza, I am so happy to finally meet you! Danny's told me all about you!"

"Has he?" I asked, wondering just how well informed his family actually was.

"You know how Danny's a chatterbox," Alicia said, "but he didn't mention how beautiful you are."

"I said she's gorgeous," Dan said.

"Not this gorgeous," Alicia shot back, then she pulled me in for the biggest bear hug. "Aww, I'm so happy you're here!"

"I'm happy too." I patted Alicia's back, while Dan grinned at us. "You said we got here in the nick of time?"

Alicia stepped back from me, and said, "Oh, it's awful. Ma and Nonna got in a fight, and then Carmelo and Joey took all the kids to the park, and now I don't know what's going to happen."

Dan crossed his arms over his chest. "What's the fight about?"

"Nonna wants to make fried calamari tonight, but Ma wants to have it on Christmas Eve," Alicia replied.

"You can't have calamari on both days?" I asked, emphasis on the *you*. There was no way I was eating fried squid bits for dinner. Dan and Alicia both looked at me like I'd grown a new head.

"Both days?" Alicia shook her head. "That won't work."

"Will it be a calamari catastrophe?" I asked, and Alicia giggled.

"Danny, I like her," Alicia said, to Dan's obvious relief. "Come on. I need you to smooth things over with Ma while I show Eliza the wine cabinet."

Before I could protest, Alicia looped her arm with mine and led me deeper into the house, with Dan trailing close behind us. As we passed the stairs, I heard a scream come from the floor above. Since Alicia didn't react, I assumed it was a spirit, and, thanks to years of practice ignoring supernatural occurrences while in mundane situations, I kept a straight face. But Dan heard it, too.

"What was that?" Dan demanded. "Who's upstairs?"

"No one," Alicia replied. "Ma's in the dining room, and Nonna's downstairs. Other than the five of us, no one else is home."

Dan nodded, then he looked at me and shrugged. If he and I both heard the scream, but no one else did, that confirmed it was a spirit. I sighed, and realized my seer abilities would be needed right here in his family's house.

Merry Christmas to me.

My tour of the wine cabinet began with Alicia showing me around the living room. It was a large space, with a sunken conversation pit in the center of the room that was straight out of the seventies. Behind the conversation pit was a built in wine cooler. Alicia pulled a bottle out of the cooler and poured me a very full glass of Chardonnay.

"Unless you'd prefer red," Alicia said, as an afterthought. "I just figured white was a good choice, since it's still daytime."

"White is great," I said, as I accepted the cold glass. The glass hadn't been chilled beforehand; the entire house was cold, as if someone forgot to pay the heating bill. And for the record, I had never drunk different colors of wine or anything else based on the time of day. Must be a New York thing. "Thank you," I said, as I sipped the wine.

"You are so welcome," Alicia said, as she emptied out the bottle into her glass. "Come on. I'll show you the dining room, and you can meet Ma."

We entered the dining room, which was even larger than the living room. This house was turning out to be positively palatial. The dining room was dominated by a long wooden table surrounded by a dozen chairs, with more pushed up against the far wall. Based on the size of the house and the ample seating, I was beginning to wonder if Dan was related to everyone in Queens.

Speaking of Dan, he was standing in front of the table and next to a woman who looked like an older version of him. She had the same dark eyes and dark curly hair, and, based on the way she was scowling at Dan, they had matching tempers, too.

"They look happy," I murmured.

"It always starts this way," Alicia replied. "Ma gets mad, then her and Danny argue a bit, then he calms her down. It'll be good. You'll see." Alicia took a breath and squared her shoulders, then she approached them. "Ma, look! Eliza's here!"

Dan's mother looked toward us, and her scowl deepened. Great. "Alicia, you gave her wine before you took her coat? Who raised you?"

"Sorry, Ma," Alicia said, as her mother grabbed the glass from my hand and set it on the table, then she manhandled me out of my leather jacket.

"Poor thing will collapse from heat stroke if she keeps this coat on," Dan's mother said. Actually, hypothermia was more of an imminent danger in this frigid house, but I kept that observation to myself. "I'm Patty, by the way," she added.

"I'm Eli, but you knew that." Patty forced a smile and thrust my glass toward me. As she did, she caught sight of the tattoos scattered across my forearms. Thanks to my father's work as the seers' marksman, I had quite the collection of protection sigils, along with the bright blue seer's mark on my wrist.

"Aren't you colorful," Patty said as she draped my jacket over the back of a chair. "None of my children have tattoos."

"But I want one," Alicia chimed in.

Dan cleared his throat. "I have one."

Patty's eyes widened. "You do? Oh, my God. Show it to me! No, wait, don't." She shook out her hands. "I don't want to know. Anyway, like I said, Nonna's being totally unreasonable. You should go talk to her."

"I'm talking to you," Dan said.

"I can talk to Nonna," I offered, since it looked like there was a lot more was going on between Dan and his mother than a discussion about a dinner menu, and I was the outsider. "Is she in the downstairs kitchen?"

Patty regarded me. "She is. Before you go, Eliza, tell me what you think about us having calamari for dinner tonight?"

"Being that I don't cook, I always leave the menu choices to those that do," I replied. No way was I taking a side before I understood the stakes. "I'm sure anything you make will be delicious."

Patty nodded, then she indicated the far side of the room. "Good answer. The stairs are there."

"I'll be down in a minute," Dan said. I flashed him a smile, then I crossed the room and went down to the basement kitchen.

Based on the room's description, I'd expected it to be a kitchen in a basement. In reality, there was a whole second house nestled downstairs, with a dining room and full bathroom right off the stairs, while the kitchen was at the end of a short hallway. The bottom floor was set up more like an in-law apartment than a basement, which was nice. I liked it when people took care of their elders.

I stood in the kitchen doorway, and saw a woman bustling around over the stove. She had dark hair pinned up under a bright blue scarf, and was wearing a navy blue housedress and slippers. Since I didn't want to startle her, I knocked on the doorframe.

"Si?" she said as she turned to face me. "Chi sei?"

"Io sono Eliza," I replied, then I switched to English. "I'm here with Dan."

"Ah. The new wife." Nonna pointed toward the stools lined up at the counter. "Sit, and I feed you. You speak Italian?"

"Only a little," I said as I took a seat. "My best friend is from Italy. She taught me some."

Nonna's head bobbed. "What part of Italy?"

"Apulia," I replied. "She lived on a farm that had orange groves."

"Ah," Nonna said with a smile. "To live in the sun like that is a good life. You always have wine before dinner?"

"Oh, no." I pushed my glass away. In reality, I hardly drank at all, since alcohol tended to mess with my foresight. The last things I needed to deal with were inaccurate predictions and meaningless visions. "Alicia gave it to me. She was so excited, and I didn't want to say no."

"Alicia is a good girl." Nonna confiscated my glass and set it next to the stove. "You like coffee?"

"I love coffee!"

Nonna laughed, then she returned to the counter with two cups of coffee. After she set them down, she brought over a platter of biscotti.

"This better than wine, no?"

"Definitely." I grabbed a biscotti and dunked it in my coffee. "Thank you."

"You a seer?"

I froze with my biscotti mid-dunk. "How did you know?"

She jerked her chin toward my left wrist. "You mark," she replied, then she laid her left arm palm up on the counter. In the same location I was marked, Nonna had a tattoo of her own. Instead of being an abstract bit of circles and lines like mine was, her mark was a stylized fleur-de-lis. "I get mine in Benevento on my sixteenth birthday."

"Dan has a mark, too," I said, since I obviously didn't need to keep supernatural secrets from Nonna. "I gave it to him, so he could sense magic. What's up with the mad spirit upstairs?"

Nonna sighed. "That my husband. He love attention, but I tell everyone to ignore him."

"Dan's grandfather is trapped in the house?"

"Oh, no, he no related to Danny. Upstairs is my first husband."

Chapter Two
The Legendary Lyons Charm

I watched Eli disappear down the stairs to Nonna's kitchen, wishing I could go with her. But Nonna was a sweetheart, and Eli could take care of herself. Besides, I needed to handle one situation at a time. After one last glance at the stairs, I faced my mother.

"You could have been a little nicer to Eli," I said.

"You could have been a little more forthcoming about getting married again," Ma retorted. "Maybe invite your mother to the wedding?"

"The wedding was small," I said. "And it wasn't really a wedding. Everything happened pretty fast."

"Why so fast?" Ma asked. "Did you two get drunk in Vegas and go to one of those tourist chapels?"

"No, but that would have been fun." When Ma narrowed her eyes at me, I continued, "We were visiting some of Eli's relatives, and one of them performs handfastings. I'd never heard of one, so I asked him a few questions about it. Turns out, it's basically a marriage ceremony. Later on, I asked Eli how she felt about getting handfasted, and she said yes. So, we did it."

"That's it?" Ma demanded. "Is this even legal?"

I shrugged. "It's more of a declaration of intent, where the couple chooses how long they want to stay together."

"And what did you two declare?" Ma asked.

"We declared that we would remain a couple forever," I replied; when I closed my eyes, I could still see Eli smiling up at me as she said she'd take forever with me. "We both chose forever."

"That's so romantic," Alicia said, as she clasped her hands over her heart. I glanced at her wineglass and wondered how much of that stuff she'd had. "So it was love at first sight, and then you whisked her away for a handfasting."

"It was not exactly love at first sight," I said. "Eli and I have known each other for a long time. It was years before she'd give me the time of day."

"What changed her mind?" Ma asked.

I spread my arms wide and grinned. "The legendary Lyons charm, of course."

Alicia laughed, and Ma scoffed. "Real charming, Danny," Ma said, then she walked toward the kitchen. "Did you eat yet? Or have you come here starved as usual?"

"We ate before we left." If Ma was trying to feed me, she wasn't mad any longer. I hoped. "Why, did you cook something?"

Ma stopped walking and glared at me over her shoulder. "Daniel Edward Lyons, sit down so I can make you a plate."

I sat at the kitchen table as ordered, even though that was where the kids ate. Yeah, I saw what she was doing there. "I'm sorry you weren't there when we had the ceremony. Eli and I made a spur of the moment decision. We weren't trying to exclude anyone."

Ma harrumphed, then she set a roast beef sandwich in front of me. "Regardless of how it happened, I'm glad you found someone. Everyone deserves to find their partner, and be happy." She paused, and asked, "You're sure about Eliza?"

"I am, Ma," I said. "From the first moment I saw her, I was sure."

Ma smiled and ducked her head. "That's wonderful. Now I just need to find partners for your sisters."

"Good luck with that," I said, but I really only meant that comment toward the older two. Alicia was kind and intelligent and told great jokes, and anyone would be lucky to be with her. Theresa and Dolores were in their own world. I saw a flat of plants sitting on the floor near the back door. "Is that this year's crop of mistletoe?"

"It is. We picked it up yesterday."

Sandwich in hand, I wandered over to the flat and had a peek inside. Laying in neat little rows were dozens of bundles of mistletoe, each one tied with a red ribbon and decorated with a sparkling glass flower. My mother loved to decorate for Christmas, and she made a big deal about keeping all of the decorations up until a week after New Year's Day. Yeah, we were that house, with the ten miles of colored lights in the yard and an animatronic Frosty the Snowman on the front lawn. There used to be a Santa Claus display that went up on the roof, but a few of my brothers destroyed that years ago during a prank gone wrong. Ma could never figure out who the responsible party was, which was the only reason she hadn't tanned the main perpetrator's hide. Instead, when we wouldn't rat out the one who came up with that caper, we were all grounded for a month.

Suddenly, something glinted from inside the flat of mistletoe. I pushed the plants aside, searching for the source of the light, and realized that each bundle was glowing with the unmistakable aura of magic.

"Do you think Eliza is all right downstairs with Nonna?" Ma asked, rousing me from my investigation of the plants.

"I'm sure she's fine," I replied. "Eli gets along with everyone. She flashes that thousand watt smile of hers, and people start telling her their life stories. Eli wears her heart on her sleeve, and people sense how good she is. I've never met anyone who wasn't charmed by her."

Ma stopped was she was doing and smiled at me. "You really love her."

"Yeah," I said, as I picked one of the mistletoe sprigs and twirled it around my fingers. Magic swirled around it like a trail of red light. "I really do."

"I'm sure she and I will get along just fine," Ma said. "We just need to get to know each other." My mother patted my arm, then she returned to whatever she had going on the stove. I set down the mistletoe, and frowned. Strong magic was emanating from each one of these plants, but who would enchant a bunch of mistletoe? My mother had been getting her mistletoe from the same farm every year since she'd gotten married. Had the mistletoe always been soaked in magic, or was this new?

I finished my sandwich, then I put my plate in the dishwasher. "I'm going to check on Eli."

"Miss her already?" Ma teased.

"You know it," I replied, and while that was true, I had a secondary motive. If these plants were enchanted, Eli would know what to do. No one understood poisonous plants better than my wife.

Chapter Three
Drama Llama

After I got over the initial shock of Nonna being a seer, and that she was all right with her first husband's ghost screaming up a storm from the second floor, we had a great time chatting. She told me stories about how Dan and his siblings used to run amok as children, and how Dan was always the peacemaker between everyone, even the older kids. He also ran interference between his mother and the rest of the family, and, according to Nonna, they'd sorely needed him the past few years.

"Patty, she mean well, but she can be a little much," Nonna said. "You need to let the kids make their own mistakes. It how we all learn."

"I hear ya," I said, as I thought about some of my own mistakes. I'd made some real whoppers over the years, but I wouldn't say they taught me anything useful, except for the importance of hiding the evidence. "So how many seers are out here in Queens? Do you have a community?"

"No like we had in the old country," Nonna replied. "When I first come here there were a few witches in the neighborhood, but they moved on."

"Interesting." The more I thought about Dan's grandmother being a seer, the more it made sense. Dan had amazing intuition, and the seer's mark I'd tattooed on him had given him an extreme sensitivity to magic I hadn't anticipated. If he'd had some supernatural blood in him all along, that explained a few things.

Speaking of Dan, he was still upstairs with his mother and sister. "How do you think it's going up there with the three of them?"

Nonna shrugged, and made a noncommittal gesture. "Patty will pretend she mad or sad, and it will be up to Danny to snap her out of it. Then everything be fine."

I leaned across the counter and said, "Patty sounds like a drama llama."

Nonna burst into laughter. "She is llama," she agreed, then she got up and made her way toward the stove. I hadn't moved since Nonna had offered me a seat at the counter, but she got up every few minutes to check the pots on the stove, or refill our coffee cups and bring over more cookies or other treats. After all of those refills, I was so caffeinated I could hear color. "Patty try her best, though. She loves her babies. Sometimes I think she love Danny most of all."

"He is pretty lovable." I stirred my spoon in my coffee, and watched all the biscotti crumbs get swept up in a tiny whirlpool. "But you knew that."

"I did." Nonna returned to her seat across the counter, and held out her hand. After a moment, I realized she wanted to see my rings. I set my hand in hers, and watched as she scrutinized my jewelry. One was a plain white gold band that matched Dan's, while the other had an oval sapphire surrounded by tiny white diamonds.

"Danny pick these out for you?" she asked.

"Actually, that is a really long story," I replied. "The short version is that the rings found us."

"Happens to our kind," she said, as she patted and then released my hand. "That how you know the gods approve. They start leaving things in your path."

"Really." I never considered that these rings—which we'd found in our closet while trapped in an alternate reality—were a gift from a higher power. When we had come across them, I'd been so concerned with fixing the broken timeline I hadn't thought much about them at all. "Is that how you met your husband? Did the gods send you a sign?"

She laughed softly. "If anything, they send a warning."

Before I could ask why she'd needed a warning, I heard someone coming down the stairs. Without turning around, I knew it was Dan.

"My two favorite girls," he said, when he entered the kitchen. "Nonna, I don't know what you're cooking but it smells great!" He kissed his grandmother's cheek, then he came around the counter and pulled up a stool next to me. "You two getting to know each other?"

"Eliza speak Italian," Nonna said, with a knowing look. "We get along just fine."

"Nonna gave me coffee," I said. "And biscotti!"

"I told you, she's an empress down here." Dan had no sooner said the words than Nonna brought him a cup of coffee. "Grazie, Nonna."

"I have never heard you speak a word of Italian before," I said, as I grabbed my third biscotti.

"I save it up for when I'm home." He drank some coffee. "Alicia's got Ma distracted up there. She really liked you."

I almost asked if he meant his sister or his mother, but I feared I already knew the answer to that. "Alicia said the rest of your family went to a park?"

"Some are at the park, some went shopping." He fidgeted with his cup and saucer. "They'll all be here soon."

I scooted closer to him, and laid my head on his shoulder. "Remember, no matter what happens today or any day, your mother will always win over my mother. Always."

He laughed softly, and kissed my hair. "Yeah, there's that."

Nonna watched the two of us and smiled. "Look at you two. Such love. Now, you eat." She turned to the stovetop and began wrestling a huge stockpot off the burner. Dan leapt to his feet and was at her side in an instant.

"Whoa, Nonna, let me help," he said, but she shooed him away.

"You know Nonna strong," she said. "You can get bowls."

Dan did as ordered and retrieved a stack of bowls from the cabinet. Nonna ladled food into each bowl, and had Dan bring them over to the counter.

"What's this?" I asked, hoping it wasn't fishy.

"Tortellini en brodo," Nonna replied. "You eat now, Eliza."

"Yes, ma'am." Our bowls appeared to be filled with pasta in a clear broth without a speck of squid, and I was cool with that. I spooned up some broth, and sipped. It was good, fragrant and not too salty.

Dan dropped his spoon. I looked toward him as spots danced before my eyes. I remember noticing that the spots were gold, instead of the usual black that heralded an upcoming loss of consciousness, and how pretty they were. Then I was out.

Chapter Four
Threads and Visions

When I opened my eyes, I was on the astral plane. I was alone, without Dan or Nonna's spirits nearby, or even my lunch. My spirit had been set adrift in a basement kitchen run by a seer from the old country.

"Is she a seer, or a witch," I muttered. Either way, I'd been eating her biscotti and drinking her coffee willy nilly, heedless of whatever poisons or spells she could be putting in the food. Hell, that soup could have been crafted to make me meet my ancestors, and who knows what was in the wine Alicia handed me.

Since I wasn't going to learn anything sitting around, I got up and did a bit of exploring. The kitchen had that gray cast that was prominent in dreams and visions, which made me wonder why Nonna had sent me to an alternate plane, when telling me whatever she wanted me to know would have been easier and faster. I rubbed the back of my neck, trying to force information from my foresight. It tingled a bit but didn't offer up any clues. Typical.

I found a set of French doors that led out of the kitchen and into the side yard. I pushed the doors open, and was surprised at the warm air in the yard. I followed the unseasonably lush lawn around the corner, and found a greenhouse. Inside it was packed with summer vegetables: tomatoes, peppers, and green and yellow squash, all healthy and ripe for the picking. Whoever was running this greenhouse had the greenest thumb in town, since it wasn't easy to grow these plants out of season. I remembered the greenhouse Charlotte had set up in Dan's yard a few years ago, and couldn't ignore the similarities. Following a hunch, I brushed aside a few tomato leaves, and saw a fat belladonna stem creeping up the back wall.

"This is all a little strange," I said, out loud. "Who grows belladonnas with tomatoes?"

A tall, bearded man appeared behind me, and grinned. "They're all in the same family."

I gasped and sat straight up, thankfully back in my physical body. Dan was still asleep next to me with his head resting on the counter. Nonna was nowhere to be found.

"Dan? Dan!" I shook his shoulder a bit more violently than necessary, but we'd both just been poisoned. I needed to know if he was okay. "Dan!"

"I'm here," he grumbled. "My head is killing me."

"Yeah, well." I stood up and scoped out the room, ensuring we were alone. "Poison'll do that." I approached the stove, and started opening and smelling the jarred spices Nonna had laid out on the counter.

"Poison?" he repeated. "All we had was Nonna's soup." I glanced at him over my shoulder, then I resumed my investigation. "Wait, you think Nonna poisoned us?"

"Did you know your grandmother is a seer?" There was nothing incriminating in the jars next to the stove, so I moved on to the cabinets.

"She is not." Dan stood next to me at the counter. "What are we looking for?"

"She recognized my seer's mark, and showed me hers. You never noticed your grandmother's tattoo?"

"She always said it was from when she was young, never acted like she wanted to talk about it." Dan watched me root through the spice cabinet. "And she's not really my grandmother."

I set down the jar of turmeric I'd just opened. "What?"

"We think she's my great-grandmother, but she might be an aunt," Dan replied.

"You think? You don't know?"

"No one knows when she came to this country, and she doesn't have a birth certificate. The only identification she ever had was her marriage license. She doesn't even have a bank account."

"Dan." I took a deep breath, and asked, "What sort of people do we interact with who live exceedingly long lives, and tend to eschew modern technology?"

He frowned. Hard. "Well, this sucks."

I pulled him into my arms. "Maybe not. Maybe it's just new information, and we only need to figure it out. We're good with figuring stuff out, right?"

"Yeah, we are. Also, there's more."

"More what?"

"Ma got some decorations delivered to the house. They're soaked in magic."

I sighed. "Of course they are. Let's table that for now, and work on one thing at a time."

"Whatever you say, baby." Dan squeezed me, then he kissed my forehead before he stepped back and surveyed the countertop. "Kind of rude that Nonna poisoned you when you first met."

I shrugged. "Seers poison each other all the time. It's how we get to know one another." I paused, and said, "And she sent me a vision. I went into a greenhouse, and a man was growing tomatoes and belladonnas."

"You and your poison gardens." Dan went to the French doors on the far side of the kitchen and looked out into the yard. "Greenhouse is shut down for the winter."

"Not surprising," I muttered. I came across a stoppered glass vial filled with a clear liquid. I pulled out the stopper and sniffed, expecting an herbal or perhaps even a minty scent. Nothing.

Hmm. Some poisons pretend to be nothing, when they're really something.

"Dan."

"Yeah, babe?"

"Do you happen to know Nonna's name?"

"Of course I do. It's Esme Tofana."

I set the stopper back in the vial. "You've got to be kidding me."

After I explained to Dan that Giulia Tofana had been an infamous seventeenth century poison queen, and that his dear sweet Nonna had likely poisoned us with the Tofana proprietary blend of arsenic, lead, and belladonna, we put the spice cupboard back together and went upstairs. We soon learned that Dan's siblings were back from the park and their shopping expeditions, along with all the spouses and nieces and nephews.

"Why didn't we hear them?" Dan muttered. "There isn't even a door on the stairs."

"There's probably a silencing spell on the stairs, so Nonna can work undisturbed," I muttered back. "Hey, think Nonna randomly tossing poisons in the food is why your mom's so uptight?"

Dan glared at me. "Later," he said, then a few of his relatives spotted him.

"Danny," one man yelled, then he and two others attacked Dan with a series of shoulder claps and awkward man hugs. "Where's the new bride?"

"Her name is Eliza, and she's right here," Dan said as he extricated himself from them. He slid his arm around my waist, and said, "Eli, these are my brothers, Carmelo, Joey, and Frank Junior."

"Hello," I said, with a wave. "Nice to meet all of you." Apparently, what I said was hilarious, because they all burst into laughter. I glanced at Dan, but he only shook his head.

"Don't try to understand," he said. "This crew makes no sense." He noticed a woman on the far side of the room, and called, "Hey, Theresa!"

The woman turned around. When she saw Dan's hand on my back she grabbed another woman's arm and they looked me up and down.

I did the same, and noted their permed brown hair and matching sweaters. The two of them whispered furiously for a bit, then they approached us.

"I'm Theresa, and this is Dolores," the first woman—Theresa—said.

"It's Lori, actually," Dolores said, with a glare at Theresa. "Only old ladies go by Dolores. You must be Eliza. We're Danny's older sisters."

"Hi," I said, but without the wave that time. Those two were not friendly, and I couldn't wait to ask Dan what their deal was. "It's great to meet all of you."

"Did you come by yourself?" Theresa asked.

"I came with Dan," I said, but Dolores shook her head.

"What she means is, did you bring any of your family up with you?" Dolores asked.

"No, I didn't," I replied. "I don't have a big family. It's really just my dad and me." I wondered how my father and Tessa were getting along, alone together for the holidays. They both claimed they didn't care about the holiday season, but I caught Tessa looking for decorations in the basement. I had a feeling that by Christmas Eve, the house would end up covered in tinsel from top to bottom.

"Not even any sisters? That sounds boring," Dolores said, then she turned to Dan. "Good job making Ma happy again."

"Yeah," Theresa said. "Maybe Eliza will let you come home more often so you can keep her relaxed."

Right after Theresa casually dropped that comment, there was a commotion on the far side of the room involving some of the kids. Dan's sisters went to investigate, though I didn't know if their kids were involved. Hell, I didn't even know if those two had any kids, and I had yet to meet any of the siblings' significant others. At this rate, I would need to start writing down names and relationships.

"Don't listen to Theresa," Dan said, once his sisters were out of earshot. "She does a lot of talking, but not a lot of thinking."

"It's okay. Meeting new people can be stressful." I'd made my share of awkward small talk over the years, so I could overlook anything his sisters said. Besides, we lived hours away. It's not like I would have to deal with them often. "I like how everyone calls you Danny."

He smiled ruefully. "They like to remind me I'm the almost youngest. I like to remind them that I'm the best looking."

"And the most modest," I added. "Is your father here?"

"He's gotta be here somewhere," Dan said, then he pointed toward the dining room. "There he is, standing with Ma."

I looked toward the dining room's entryway, and saw a man who appeared to be in his sixties standing next to Patty. He resembled the man from my vision, but I hadn't gotten a good enough look at the person in the greenhouse to be certain it was the same guy. Then the back of my neck prickled, and my foresight flared to life. I braced myself for a vision, but it didn't come. Instead, my foresight pulled out a new trick, and manifested itself as seven golden threads.

The threads originated at Dan's father, and one stretched to each of his children. As I contemplated what these threads meant for Dan, I noticed a red glow emanating from the ceiling. Hanging above Dan's parents was a kissing ball made of fresh mistletoe, and it was going out of its way to get my attention. Nonna appeared at my side, and nodded toward the threads.

"Now you know what I need to show you," she said, then she disappeared into the kitchen.

Chapter Five
Back In It

We left Nonna's place soon after Eli had been introduced to everyone. Meeting that many new people at once could be overwhelming, and while Eli hadn't complained about any of it, I didn't want to stress her out. I was stressed enough for both of us, what with the revelation that Nonna was a seer, and that she had casually poisoned us. And what the hell was going on with the mistletoe?

"What's wrong?" I asked, once we were in the car. Eli hadn't said a word in at least ten minutes, except to say goodbye to my parents.

"There you go with your famous intuition," she said. "Now that we know you're descended from seers, it all makes sense."

"But I'm not a seer. Am I?" I shook my head. "Babe, I really need to hold you."

"I know." She wound her arm around mine. "Soon."

When we got to the hotel, we checked in and went straight up to our room. We'd debated getting a room in a bed and breakfast, but in the end we opted for the total privacy of a standard hotel chain. After spending the afternoon with my large and loving yet boisterous family, I knew we'd made the right choice.

Eli set her suitcase next to the television stand, and faced me. "Want to talk?"

"Later," I said, as I wrapped my arms around her and pulled her onto the bed. We stayed like that for a few minutes, her cheek against my throat and my face buried in her hair, and for a short time, all was right in our world. Then Eli began sharing what was on her mind.

"Nonna showed me something when we were upstairs with your family," she said. "She's on your dad's side, right?"

"Yeah." I pushed myself up onto my elbow. "What did she show you? And when did this happen?"

"It was a leftover from whatever she poisoned us with," she began, then she described a set of shimmering gold threads that tethered my father to all seven of his kids. Eli concluded by telling me about the unusual red glow that came from the mistletoe.

"Those kissing balls are Ma's thing," I said. "Every year she goes out to the same farm and gets a bunch of mistletoe, which this year seems to be magical. It's poisonous, right?"

"Yeah, but it's a pretty weak poison. It will make you feel a bit nauseous, but that's it."

"Not like what Nonna put in the soup," I said. "This Giulia Tofana you mentioned. She killed a lot of people?"

"Around six hundred victims are known."

I blew out a breath. "This is… this is nuts."

"Tell me about it." Eli tugged open my shirt's buttons. "What do you think about the threads from the mistletoe?"

"I really don't know what to think," I replied. "But the memory that keeps popping up in my mind is Ma's stories about how her and Dad married young, and she wanted kids right away. It took a while though, then bam! She had all seven of us in less than ten years."

"Holy cow, that's a lot of kids in a decade!"

"Sure is." I flopped onto my back and draped my arm across my eyes. "You know how you asked why Ma is so uptight? And I'm sure you noticed how everyone wants you to 'let' me come home more often."

"I noticed." Eli moved closer to me and slid her arm around my waist. "You don't have to tell me if it's too much."

I turned toward her and kissed her forehead. "It's not too much. Anyway, it's pretty obvious my parents had some kind of fertility treatment."

"Like, the best treatment in the history of treatments," Eli said.

"You're right about that. Fast forward a bunch of years. I started seeing Charlotte—who couldn't have kids—and Ma started haranguing her about getting some kind of treatment so she could get pregnant, and they ended up having a confrontation. Her and Ma never saw eye to eye after that."

"Wow. Charlotte had some balls to stand up to your mother like that."

"She sure did," I said, with a small laugh. Char was a firecracker, no doubt about that. "You see, Ma's big complaint about me and Char wasn't just that we'd never be able to have kids together. Char had also been married before. Eventually Char had enough and told Ma she cared more about appearances than her own family." Dan glanced at me. "Char hit the nail on the head with that one."

"Go Charlotte," Eli said. "Have I ever told you that you have great taste in women?"

"According to Ma, I'm batting a hundred," I said. "She's waiting to see if she can get along with you."

"She sure loved my tattoos," Eli said. "Did you show her your mark?"

"I did not. I know better than to cause a scene at the holidays."

"Danny the peacemaker," Eli said. "Now that I'm up to date on the family drama, we need to figure out why Nonna wanted me to know about all the Lyons family history. It's not like any of this directly affects me."

"And she couldn't have wanted you to tell me, because I already knew," I concluded. "You think there's a supernatural reason?"

"Could be," Eli replied. "Do you know anything about Nonna's husband? Maybe he was a witch, or a seer." She threaded her fingers through the hair at the nape of my neck, which I loved. When her fingernails gently scraped my scalp, it sent little shocks down my spine. "Or something else."

"Something else?" I drew back and regarded my wife. "What the hell else is there?"

"All sorts of shit."

I blew out another breath, then I gathered Eli against me. "Looks like you're back in it, Mistress of Seers."

Eli clenched her fist against my chest. "Believe me, no matter what I do, I always get dragged back into it."

Chapter Six
Maple Acres

The next morning dawned clear and sunny. It was also cold enough to freeze windshield wiper fluid.

"Good day to play football," Dan said, as he surveyed the frozen world outside the hotel's window and I hid under the down comforter. "Or go ice skating."

"Is that what New Yorkers do in winter?" I asked. "Where I come from, we stay inside when it's below freezing."

"What can I say. New Yorkers are tough." He got back in bed, and I tried not to mention his cold hands. At least he was wearing socks. "What do you want to do today?"

"You don't have to meet up with your family?"

"Maybe for dinner. Before that, it's all about me and you, baby." He nuzzled my neck. "We could go out for breakfast. There's a diner my buddy's family owns. I used to hit it up all the time. After we eat, I can show you around the neighborhood, all my old haunts. Or we could stay right here," he suggested, as the nuzzling became nibbling.

I stretched my neck for more kisses. He obliged. "All of those sound like great ideas."

"All? Does one of them sound more enjoyable than the rest? Maybe an option that involves you being naked and us ordering room service?"

I flipped Dan onto his back, climbed on top of him, and demanded, "Are you trying to keep me from having yummy diner pancakes?" His eyes widened, then he laughed. Dan was a lot bigger and stronger than me, and I'd only been able to flip him over because he went along with it. "Not cool, Lyons."

"I would never stand between you and pancakes, Mrs. Lyons," he said, and I felt my cheeks warm. We weren't officially married, and I hadn't changed my name, but whenever he referred to me as Mrs. Lyons, I blushed like a schoolgirl. Dan made no secret of how much he liked that. "I take it we're getting out of bed, then."

"We can stay in bed at home." Despite my words, I made no move to get up. "After you take me out for breakfast, I think we should talk about the mistletoe."

"That is definitely a discussion to b had on a full stomach," he said. "Remember when I mentioned the decorations soaked in magic?"

"And?"

"That was the mistletoe. There's so much magic on them they practically glow."

I wondered how Dan could have forgotten to mention that rather significant detail, but he was still new to magic. That, and he'd already handled a lot of new information after all that had happened yesterday. "I say if the magic mistletoe wants to talk, we should listen. Wait, I know what we should do today."

Dan gave me a sly grin as his hand slid down to my thigh. "Really."

"Not that. Well, not just that. Can we go up to the farm where your mother gets the mistletoe?"

"Seriously? That farm is in Yorktown Heights!"

"Is that far?"

As it turned out, Yorktown Heights was pretty far from Queens. Like, forty-five miles far.

But Dan loved me, and luckily he also loved driving, so after we showered and had some perfectly adequate room service pancakes, we hit the road. My diner breakfast would have to wait until tomorrow.

"Have you been to this place before?" I asked.

"Oh, yeah. We used to go out to the farm a few times a year," Dan replied. "In the fall we would go apple picking, and get some pumpkins for decorating. Then, after Thanksgiving, we would go up and pick out a Christmas tree, and Ma would get a flat of mistletoe."

"That sounds like an awful lot of mistletoe."

"It is, but she uses it up. She makes wreaths, those kissing balls like the one hanging in the dining room, and other stuff. She gives some to the neighbors, too."

I made a mental note to research why someone would want to cover their home in mistletoe. My initial thought was that Patty was setting a type of ward, but she could have been invoking a deity. Now that I knew Nonna was a seer and a Tofana, anything was possible. "Did you go to the farm at other times of the year?"

"Yeah, but not on a regular basis. We went once for my birthday. That was fun."

Dan's birthday was in March, which made me wonder if the Lyons clan had trucked up to the farm for a spring fertility rite. "What do you want for your next birthday?"

He took my hand and squeezed. "Same thing I want every day. To spend it with you."

"You must want something." Dan's next birthday would be our first together as a couple, and I wanted to do something special for him. "Maybe we can go somewhere. Or get matching tattoos."

He laughed out loud. "My wrist still hurts from the last one you gave me."

"Sure it does, tough guy. I meant real tattoos, like from a shop."

"What, you're saying mine is fake? Anyway, we're here."

Dan drove under a charming wooden archway which proudly proclaimed the establishment as Maple Acres Christmas Tree Farm. We were the only car in the lot, which surprised me. I'd assumed this place would be packed the week before Christmas. Then again, it was a Tuesday morning, which was when most regular people worked. Being that we worked for ourselves, Dan and I didn't keep regular hours, and we liked it that way.

True to its name, there were acres of evergreen trees spread out around the central parking area, although I didn't spot any maples. There were a few cute little sheds stocked with all the tools needed to chop down your own tree and bundle it up for the journey home. The wooded area seemed nice, but I was more interested in the white clapboard shop and adjacent greenhouse. That was where we would find our mistletoe, not out in the chilly wind.

Speaking of the wind, we exited the car and hunched down in our coats and scarves as icy gusts howled around us. I don't think my ears have ever been than cold, nor did I remember ever having such difficulty crossing a small parking area. It was almost as if the wind was pushing us back.

"Do you see it?" Dan asked. "There's magic in the air."

I didn't see anything, but he was the one who sensed magic, not me. "Is it friendly magic? Or like what you saw on the mistletoe?"

"Too soon to tell. After you," Dan said, as he opened the shop's door for me. I stepped inside the warm, cheery interior, and shook the blood back into my icy fingers.

"Crossing that lot was like scaling Mount Everest," I said. "Is it always this cold out here?"

"We would have it stay winter year round, if we could," came a voice from behind me. An older man wearing a blue vest edged in white fur over his jeans and flannel shirt approached us. He had a full white beard, and his nametag proclaimed him to be Ed Moroz. He'd tucked a cheery sprig of chamomile behind the tag, which was a nice touch. "Little Danny Lyons, is that you?"

"You remember me?" Dan said. "Mr. Moroz, it's been years!"

"So it has. Who's this?" he asked, with a pointed glance at me.

"Mr. Moroz, this is my wife, Eliza," Dan said. "This'll be our first Christmas together."

"Congratulations," Mr. Moroz said. "Are you here to pick out a tree?"

"Actually, I'm more interested in your mistletoe," I said. "Dan's mother raves about your product."

Mr. Moroz chuckled. "I imagine Patty does. This way. I'll show you the fresh stock."

We followed Mr. Moroz into a large florist's cooler in the rear of the shop. Behind the bouquets of roses and babies' breath was an entire wall covered with shelves of mistletoe. As if that wasn't enough, dainty clusters of the plants decorated with red velvet bows and shiny bells hung from the rafters above.

"I'm one of the few purveyors of fresh mistletoe on the east coast," Mr. Moroz proclaimed proudly. "Most stores only sell dried specimens, but not here."

I approached the shelves and had a look at the plants. They all looked healthy, and were definitely the non-native variety. I also realized that what I had thought were bells were actually tiny glass flowers affixed to each bow. "Do you only stock European mistletoe?"

"Good eye," Mr. Moroz said. "My clientele prefers the European species, so that's what I grow."

"Where are you growing it?" I asked. "This farm seems to be all evergreen, but mistletoe prefers to attach to the bark of broadleaf trees. Do you have access to another tree farm?" When Mr. Moroz's brows lowered, I added, "I'm sorry, I don't mean to be so inquisitive. I have an interest in botany."

"You have nothing to apologize for," Mr. Moroz said. "Trust our Danny to take up with a brilliant scientist. Only the best would ever do for him."

"I'm not a scientist," I said. "Actually, I'm a private investigator."

"A detective that investigates plants." Moroz smiled a bit too widely, or maybe he was baring his teeth. "Now I've heard everything."

"Gotta learn at least one new thing every day," Dan said. "I remember you selling the plants twined with another one that had red berries. What was that other plant called?"

"Holly," Moroz and I said in unison. Moroz shot me an irritated glance, before plastering on his fake smile and returning his attention to Dan.

"Yeah, that one," Dan said. "Can I get one of those arrangements for my mother?"

"Certainly," Moroz said. "I have some in the front of the shop. Right this way."

We left the cooler and went back to the sales floor. At first glance, we were in a typical floral shop, but almost every arrangement had a magical subtext. It was either an amazing coincidence, or a blatant show of power.

In my experience, those who show off how much power they possess usually turned out to be the weakest of all.

"All of the baskets have the same glass flowers," I said, as I poked one with my fingertip. Up close, I noticed the glass flowers were chamomile, like Moroz's boutonniere. "Is chamomile your favorite flower?"

"It is," he replied. "Where I'm from, the women in my family used to weave crowns of them every spring."

"That must have been pretty." I picked up a gift basket filled with mistletoe, oak branches, charcoal discs used for burning incense and herbs, and a set of elegant wooden matches. "Dendromancy?" I asked, as I held up the basket.

"Don't you know a lot about plants," Moroz said. "That interest in botany must keep you busy."

"It's not plants I'm an expert in." Since I wanted to know what Moroz's deal was, I figured I should lay all of my cards on the table. "It's poisons."

"Poisons, eh? Been a while since I saw one of your kind around here." Moroz put the gift basket in the shopping bag with the arrangement Dan picked out for his mother. "Take the basket, on the house. Let me know what you see in the smoke."

"Hey, thanks Mr. Moroz," Dan said. "I'm glad we came up today."

"As am I," Moroz said, as he offered Dan a genuine smile. "Don't be a stranger, Danny."

Dan paid for the holly arrangement, then he grabbed the shopping bag and we left the shop. The arctic blast that had pummeled us on our way in was gone, which confirmed another one of my theories. The farm was warded against seers. But why?

"That went well," Dan said when we were in the car. "Think Moroz is a witch?"

"Not sure." I took the basket out of the shopping bag and started tearing into the cellophane wrapper. "There's definitely something magical going on, but he was decidedly unhappy to have a seer on his property. Historically witches and seers work with each other, or at least try to avoid outward shows of animosity."

"He also never answered your question about where he's growing the mistletoe," Dan said.

"No, he didn't," I said. "Did you pick up on any magic in the shop?"

"The place is soaked in magic, but it's not something I've ever felt before, not even on Ma's mistletoe," he replied.

"How is it different?"

"It seems older, if that makes sense." He nodded toward the bag in my lap. "That basket. You called it dendromancy?"

"It's a type of divination where you burn an herb with a particular species of wood. You watch the smoke, and see what's revealed." I picked up the oak branch and smelled it.

"What's it smell like?" Dan asked.

"Wood. Is there someplace we can burn this?"

Dan started the truck. "I'm sure we can find a spot."

There was a hiking trail on a nearby mountain that Dan remembered visiting in the past, so that was where we went next. The foot of the mountain had a picnic area with little individual grills, which was a nice, safe way to begin our journey into dendromancy. It also beat my idea of gathering kindling and starting a fire on the ground, and possibly burning down the forest.

"All right." Dan knocked the snow off the grill, and rubbed his hands together. "What do we do first?"

"We need to get the fire going." Since we weren't going to use it again, I set the entire wicker basket on the grill and struck one of the included matches. The basket must have been sprayed with some kind of lacquer because the moment the flame touched it, it burst into flames.

"Whoa," Dan said as he pulled me back. "Maybe use newspaper to start the fire next time?"

"As you know, we don't have any newspaper." I tossed the charcoal discs on the tiny inferno I created. I didn't think we needed them, but it would be a shame to break up a set. After the flames died down a bit, Dan set the piece of oak on the fire, and I put the mistletoe on top of the wood.

"Now what?" he asked.

"Now we wait." I slid my arms underneath Dan's coat and around his waist, seeking all the warmth he could spare. Dan wrapped his arms around my shoulders and kissed my forehead. "I hate waiting."

"Yeah, me too," Dan said, then he tilted up my chin and kissed me just as passionately as he had when we were in bed earlier.

"What has gotten into you?" I asked when we parted. Dan had always been affectionate, but ever since we got to New York, he was all over me.

"I just love kissing you." I couldn't argue with that, now could I? "Looks like our smoke is congealing."

"That word conjures up some awful images," I said, then I checked out the smoke. Instead of rising and dissipating like regular smoke, ours was looping around and creating an image. It was an oval, with a smaller oval near one end. Before our eyes, the smaller orb refined itself into a face. Then the rest of the smoke arranged itself into a body and four chubby limbs.

I gasped. "That's a baby!"

"Yes, it is." Dan looked from me to the smoke and back to me, and raised an eyebrow.

"Don't get any ideas," I said. "We are not taking smoke baby home." As we watched the smoke image, it solidified into an extremely lifelike, fat, smiling baby.

"He's kinda cute."

"Yeah, he definitely takes after you." I wracked my brain for whatever information was packed in there about mistletoe, and remembered it was used to influence fertility.

"Dan, that fertility treatment you mentioned? I think your mother used mistletoe to get pregnant."

After the fire burned itself out, and Smokey the Baby blew away on the wind, we returned to the car. Dan was quiet as we walked through the snowy field, but I had dropped a bombshell on him. Now we just needed to decide what to do about it.

"How does one use mistletoe to get pregnant?" he asked, when we were inside the truck.

"In increases fertility," I replied. "If I recall correctly, mistletoe influences the man, while holly works on the woman. It's why you see them together often." I glanced at the arrangement in the back seat. "I didn't even think of the fertility aspect when you picked those plants out."

"Yeah, well, except for that story I told you earlier, I try to never think about my mother and fertility at the same time." He started the car, and turned on the heater. "Where can we get some more information about this?"

"I can ask Tess," I said, as I grabbed my phone from where I'd left it on the dashboard. I glanced at the screen, and saw a text from Dan's sister, Theresa. I'd picked up his phone by mistake. "Oh, sorry, this is yours."

I handed Dan his phone, then I grabbed mine and fired off a text to Tessa. Once that was done, I sent a second message to my dad, letting him know we were safe and happy in New York. Even though my father was a pretty mellow guy, he did worry if I didn't check in with him every few days. When both texts were out in the world, I glanced up and saw Dan frowning at the phone in his hand.

"What's wrong? Don't tell me it's more calamari drama."

"You saw the text from Theresa," he began.

"I did, but I didn't read it."

"Here." He handed me his phone. On the screen was a conversation between him and his sister that started yesterday.

"Are you sure you want me to read this?" I asked.

"Might as well know what I know," he said, as he gestured at his phone. I bit my lip, and started reading.

Theresa: Exactly how old is this Eliza?
Dan: She turned twenty-nine last September.
Theresa: Little young for you, Danny. Even Alicia's older than her.

Dan: So?

Theresa: So I knew you were lonely but cradle robbing is beneath you.

"Cradle robbing?" I asked Dan. "It's not like you were my camp counselor."

Dan rubbed his eyes. "Keep reading."

Theresa: What's this Eliza's last name?

Dan: Lyons.

Theresa: I mean her real last name.

Dan: Why do you keep calling her this Eliza? She's my wife, she's a Lyons, deal with it.

Theresa: You're not even really married.

Theresa: Though I suppose she can be more of a wife to you than Charlotte was.

Dan: Don't drag Char into this

Theresa: It's like you find these women just to upset Ma. When are you going to get a real wife?

I set down the phone. "That was enlightening. Does your entire family hate me, or just your mother and Theresa?"

"I'm so sorry," he said. "I don't know what's wrong with either of them. Any of them."

"Hey. Come here." I reached across the center console and held Dan as best I could. "Family can really suck sometimes."

"Yeah, they can." He drew back—hugging over the console in an SUV really wasn't comfortable—then he stroked his thumb across my cheekbone. "I don't care what any of them think."

"I know you don't." I understood that Dan had a hard time reconciling how much he loved his family with how they reacted to certain choices he'd made. "Now I know why you haven't been home in four years."

"Actually, you don't." He started the car, and pulled out of the parking area and headed toward the main road. "The last time I came home—which was also for Christmas—was right after Char died, and my mother and sisters decided to play matchmaker. I think I met every unattached Catholic woman on the east coast. Ever since Char passed, their mission has been to find me a new, acceptable-to-them wife."

"That must have been awful." I imagined a newly widowed Dan being forced to meet women when what he really needed was time to mourn Charlotte. "Is being Catholic one of their criteria for a real wife? Because you know I'm failing that one."

"They'll start asking you about religion on Christmas Eve. We go to midnight mass." He glanced at me. "Are you okay with going to mass? I've never seen you in a church."

"I am very okay with attending mass," I replied. "Tess and I used to attend mass at the big cathedrals in Europe."

"Really? Even though she's a witch?"

I shrugged. "Religions are just different forms of magic. We'd attend services for other religions, too."

"Huh. I never thought about it that way." He paused at a stop sign. "We've already had quite the trip. In the last day we've found out Nonna is a seer and then we got poisoned by her, you learned my mother and sisters are nuts, and now we've got some weird mistletoe to deal with."

"Actually, the mistletoe explains why you've been all over me," I said. "A part of its fertility enhancing aspect is that it increases male virility."

"Baby, mistletoe is absolutely not why I'm all over you," he said. "When we get back to our plant free hotel room, I'm going to prove it."

"Aren't we supposed to have dinner with your family tonight?"

"They can wait." He glanced at his phone, and his sister's texts. "They can wait for a long time."

Chapter Seven
Diner Pancakes

When we got back to the hotel, Dan made good on his word, and proved that no plants, holiday themed or otherwise, were influencing his affections toward me. Just to be sure, we left Moroz's holly and mistletoe arrangement in the car. I hoped the whole thing froze solid.

Hours later, I was certain that absolutely nothing would influence me to get out of bed ever again. That was when my stomach rumbled. It was so loud, Dan heard it, too.

"I guess it's dinner time," he said. "Where do you want to go?"

"Should we go to Nonna's?" I asked, then I remembered the first weird thing that happened at her house. "Actually, I think we have to go back there, or at least I should. I forgot all about the spirit on the upper floor."

"Right. That guy. Think he needs our help?"

"He was screaming," I pointed out. In my experience, screaming people, dead or otherwise, needed help. "When I asked Nonna about him, she told me he's her first husband."

Dan's eyes went wide. "First? How many have there been?"

"You can ask her those questions." I rolled onto my stomach and grabbed my phone so I could check the room service menu, and see if I'd gotten any messages. I hadn't received any responses yet from my dad or Tess, which I thought was a good sign. It must mean they were too busy pretending they didn't enjoy spending the winter holidays together to check their phones. "And how does Nonna not have any identification? How does she own the house, even?"

"It's in my father's name," Dan replied. "That's something else that Ma worries about."

"Owning a home worries her?"

"She doesn't own it. Only my father's name is on the deed."

"Shouldn't they have a calm, adult discussion about that?"

"If only." Dan set his hand on the nape of my neck, and peeked over my shoulder. "Ordering us some dinner?"

"For now, I'm just seeing what they have. I like to know what my options are." According to the hotel's site, tonight they were serving roast turkey, steak, and a vegan pasta bowl. "And these options aren't very interesting."

"Let me ask Alicia what's on at home," he said, then he paused. "Or we could go into the city, and find our own dinner."

"That sounds like fun." I tossed my phone aside. "We can be tourists. Well, I am a tourist here."

"And it's your lucky day, baby, because I am New York's best tour guide."

Our foray into the city was fun, and filled with great food, and totally exhausting.

Dan took me all around Manhattan, where we saw the massive lit up tree at Rockefeller Center, and the extravagant window displays in all the stores on Fifth Avenue. Our dinner was a few hot dogs from a street vendor that I was willing to bet tasted better than our hotel's room service steak. We had hot chocolates for dessert, then we walked through an outdoor Christmas market that reminded me of my time in Europe. It was magical, and not the sort of magic I usually dealt with. The night was damn near perfect, and I didn't want it to end.

Despite all of the exercise we got walking around the city, I still woke up early the next morning. I usually ran right after I got up, but I hadn't brought any of my gear with me. This was supposed to be a vacation, after all. Dan was snoring next to me, and it was a perfect morning to sleep in. In my version of perfection, sleeping in meant coffees in bed.

I got up to investigate the in-room coffeemaker. The included coffee grounds didn't look particularly appetizing, but I was sure they would get the job done. Once that was going, I checked my phone and saw a text from my dad.

Alex: Hey, Bug. Call me when you wake up.
Eli: Is now good?
Alex: I'm here.

I smiled, and hit call. He picked up on the first ring. "Hey, Daddy."

He chuckled; I hardly ever called him Daddy. "How's my best girl?"

"Careful. You don't want Tessa to get the wrong idea."

At that, he laughed out loud. "She knows what she means to me."

I wanted to tease him a bit about his on again, off again relationship with Tess, but he was my father. The last thing I needed was for him to divulge details I'd rather not know about. Instead, I said, "That's good. I'm glad you two are getting along."

"Me, too. Are you having a good time in New York?"

"So far, yes. As big cities go, it's no Paris or Athens, but it's got potential. Did you pick up Dan's gift?" Dan and I had agreed to exchange our gifts after we returned home, instead of hauling them all the way to New York in our luggage. Little did Dan know that I had the surprise of the century waiting for him.

"We did," Dad replied. "How is Dan's family?"

"They are quite the bunch." I poured myself a cup of complimentary hotel room coffee and sat on the window ledge. "Dan's nonna—who isn't really his grandmother—is pretty interesting. Turns out she's a seer."

"Really. That explains Dan's intuition."

"That's what I said!"

"And she's not really his grandmother? Who is she?"

"No one seems to know. She seems very old, and my guess is that enough mortals married her descendants until the supernatural aspect of her bloodline got diluted. However, the whole family revolves around her. Everyone goes to her house, she cooks special meals, the whole deal. She's even got a mark, but it's not like the ones you do."

"As marksmen, we each strive to be unique. What does her mark look like?"

"It's a fleur-de-lis."

Dad paused, then asked, "Do you know her name?"

"Get this. It's Esme Tofana."

"You have got to be kidding me. She's still around?" I heard rattling, and assumed Dad was making something in the kitchen. "Esme is Giulia's daughter, and the guardian of the family recipes. She knew your gran, too."

"Really? Did Gran like her?"

"Ma got along with everyone. Have you met any more seers?"

"Nonna said there's no seer community out here, and that all the witches moved on a while ago, but she didn't say where they went." I blew on my coffee. "She went on to feed us soup with Acqua Tofana in it, and we've also got a creepy guy selling fresh mistletoe to the masses."

"How did the Acqua Tofana go?"

"It showed me a vision of a man in a greenhouse, and there was belladonna growing with the tomatoes. Later, when we were in the dining room, the mistletoe—purchased from the aforementioned creepy man—hanging from the ceiling glowed red and shot out a bunch of gold threads."

"Interesting. Do you need me to go up there?"

"Stay with Tessa. This isn't anything we can't handle. Not yet, anyway." I thought about the Maple Acres Christmas Tree Farm, and added, "Can you ask Tess about any mistletoe lore she knows of? The farm Dan's mom buys from only sells the European species, and the guy in charge is called Moroz."

"Ded Moroz?"

"Yeah, Ed Moroz. You've met him?"
"Not Ed, Ded. He's a Slavic god of winter."
"Well, isn't that interesting."

Dad needed to hang up soon afterward—something about rolls in the oven—and as I finished my coffee, I contemplated my conversation with my father. Nonna turned out to be the daughter of one of the most famous poisoners in history, and based on her probable age, I didn't think she was Dan's great-grandmother, or even great-great-grandmother. My theory was that she had deliberately stayed close to her descendants and watched over them, which was nice. It would also explain her lack of identification, and a bank account.

However, I also recalled how Dan's father, Frank Senior, eschewed modern technology just as much as Nonna did. Many older supernatural folk liked to live in the past; my father didn't even drive. Tessa was a glaring exception to the rule, being that she owned and drove a car, had several computers and a modern cell phone, and enjoyed all aspects of living in the twenty-first century.

The more time I spent with Dan's family, the more they seemed like a family that, while maybe not supernatural themselves, had been raised by a coven of witches.

I got back into bed, and set my hand on Dan's back. I'd never thought of him as anything but my stalwart mortal who had once been the annoying police detective that haunted my every move, and was now my beloved partner. Husband. I have got to get used to calling him that.

Relationships aside, I recalled when I'd first started telling Dan the truth about myself, and that time at the apple orchard when I helped him see a ghost. It was his first ghost, and that event led to me opening up to him about my life and family. He'd readily accepted everything I told him, even though it was all new to him. Never once had he behaved like he had any knowledge of the witch or seer communities, and now I knew that he'd basically grown up in one.

Something wasn't right. Luckily for Dan, I'm good with puzzles.

"Hey." I nudged his shoulder. He opened his eyes, and smiled at me.

"Hey, beautiful." He pulled me into his arms. "What are you thinking?"

"How do you know I'm thinking anything?"

"I just do. Wanna share?"

"I talked to my dad. Your nonna knew my gran."

"Really?" Dan drew back and regarded me. "Does Nonna realize you're Helena's granddaughter?"

"I'm not sure. I only told her my name was Eliza. Since I walked away from the whole Mistress deal, I don't really want to advertise who I am."

Dan nodded. "You may have walked away, but it's pulling you back."

"Always does." I said that with more bitterness than I'd intended. Before I got too deep in my feelings, I continued, "Remember when I mentioned Giulia Tofana, the seventeenth century poison queen? According to dad, Nonna is her daughter."

"Shit." Dan rolled onto his back and draped an arm across his eyes. "Then Nonna is Tessa old."

"Nah. Tessa's been around way longer than Acqua Tofana." She'd spent time as a courtier for the first Queen Elizabeth. "I'm thinking that Nonna has been hanging out with her descendants and watching over them for... Well. For a long time."

"That sounds like Nonna."

"But what is she guarding you from?" I continued. "Oh, and your friend the mistletoe man? Dad says that Ded Moroz is a winter deity."

Dan blew out a breath. "Of course he is. Do you have any good news?"

"Yes. I got the coffeemaker to work."

We finished off the watery hotel coffee, then we headed over to Dan's favorite diner for a real breakfast. The place was called Mike's, and it was in Queens right next to one of the subway entrances. Which, I noticed, was above ground in this neighborhood.

"Aren't the subways supposed to be in tunnels?" I asked, as we walked past the stairs. "You know, for the subterranean aspect."

"You're such a tourist." Dan opened the diner's door for me, and the sweet older lady working as the hostess showed us to a booth. She brought us cups of coffee and glasses of water, and asked us what we'd like to eat.

"We haven't even seen a menu," I said, but the hostess smiled.

"We can make anything here," she promised. Dan nodded, and since this was a diner, I went for my go-to breakfast order.

"I would like some pancakes, with bacon and eggs on the side," I said. "Scrambled, please. And, do you have cereal?"

"Of course."

"Can I get a bowl of Grape Nuts, too?"

"Absolutely," she said, then she turned to Dan. "And for you, Danny?"

"Wait," I said, looking from the hostess to Dan. "You know each other?"

"Danny went to school with my youngest, Andreas," the hostess said.

"Mama Anastasia, this is my wife, Eliza," Dan said. "Sorry, babe. I wanted to surprise you."

"Nice to meet you," I said to Mama Anastasia, then I tossed Dan a glare for good measure.

"You as well," Mama replied, with a warm smile that reminded me of Dan's nonna.

"I also may have texted Andreas this morning to ask if they stocked your favorite cereal," Dan admitted.

"You are sneaky," I said. "These pancakes better be good."

"It will be the best breakfast you've ever had," Mama Anastasia promised. "You'll have your usual, Danny?"

"Sounds good," he replied, then she went to put in our order.

"I don't know about this," I said, after Mama Anastasia was out of earshot. "I'm kind of a pancake expert."

Dan reached across the table and took my hands. "Trust me, baby. You'll love them."

Dan and Mama weren't kidding. Those pancakes really were the best I'd ever had.

And it wasn't just the pancakes. The bacon and eggs and coffee were all perfect, too. Even the toast was the perfect blend of crunchy bread and rich buttery topping, and my Grape Nuts were reliably delicious. The food was so good it made me wonder if the kitchen was stocked with enchanted cooking pots.

Hm. Maybe I could get Tess to come over for breakfast, and enchant a frying pan or two.

After we'd eaten so much food we could barely move, Dan went up to pay, but Mama refused his money.

"Mama, you can't just give away meals," Dan said.

"You can repay me by coming in more often," Mama said. "Eliza, you'll make sure he comes back to visit me?"

"I will, Mama," I said, as my foresight sparked. There was something magical about her, too, and we would run into each other sooner than later. "Promise."

Mama patted my hand. "You're a good girl. I look forward to seeing you both again."

We left the diner warm and happy and feeling all the emotions that honestly we should have gotten from Nonna's house. The only members of the Lyons family that had been happy to see us were Nonna, and Alicia. Since I didn't want to ruin our morning by bringing up the lukewarm reception we'd received, I asked Dan about our surroundings.

"Is this the neighborhood you used to hang around in as a young troublemaker?" I asked.

"It sure is. Mama Anastasia's son, Andreas, and I went to school a few blocks away, and I used to work at that bakery." He pointed to a storefront across the street.

"Let me guess, you were the cake decorator?"

"They knew better than to let me near the food. I delivered bread at the crack of dawn on my bike."

"That must have been fun."

"I don't know about fun, but it paid well, and they gave me all the bread and cakes I could eat. It was a good job while I was in high school."

"Did any of your other siblings work there?"

"Frank Junior did for a bit, but he didn't like getting up early. I didn't like getting up early either, but I liked having my work over with before noon on the weekends." We reached a corner, and waited for the light to turn. "Frank Junior's always wanted to impress our older brothers. He didn't want to hang out with little ol' me."

"That's his loss, because you're awesome." The light turned, and we crossed. "So, Frank Junior is brother number three?"

"Yeah. It goes Theresa, Carmelo, Joey—his name's Giuseppe, but we've always called him Joey—Dolores, Frank, me, and then Alicia."

"If Carmelo's the oldest boy, why isn't he Frank Junior? Isn't that sort of naming convention reserved for the eldest son?"

"Carmelo is Ma's father's name, and Dad's father was Giuseppe," Dan replied. "Dad had to wait for the third son to get a namesake."

"If you think we're having three kids just to get to a Dan Junior, you're nuts," I said. "The first one can be Daniel Alexander Frank. Or, Danielle Alexandra Francesca." Suddenly, I realized what sort of words were falling out of my mouth. "N-Not that we're having any kids."

Dan looped his arm around my shoulders and kissed my cheek. "Whatever you say, baby."

Chapter Eight
Like Calls To Like

Dan showed me a few more of his favorite places from when he was younger, then we went to Nonna's house. According to Dan, she liked to serve big lunches for the entire family, so we would arrive while she was in the middle of cooking. That meant we would not only get to enjoy some snacks while she cooked, Nonna would be alone in her kitchen so we could ask her anything.

"Your mother never helps her cook?" I asked, as Dan turned onto Nonna's street.

"Nah. They each stay in their respective kitchens. That's why Nonna does lunch, and Ma does dinner."

"Who does breakfast? And is it weird to have your mother and grandmother cooking on different floors, like dueling kitchens? That's got to be awkward with just your parents and Nonna living there."

"Alicia, Theresa, and Dolores are there, too. Everyone lives at home until they get married."

"And only you and your brothers have ever been married?"

"Yeah." Dan's voice held a note of surprise, as if he was just noticing the rather big family divide happening right under his nose. "Theresa was engaged once, but nothing came of it."

"Have Alicia or Dolores ever had a serious relationship?"

"Alicia's had a pretty serious one that started in high school, but it's been off for a while now," Dan replied. "As for Dolores, no one wants to put up with her for very long except Theresa."

"And you're the only one who ever moved away," I murmured. "Why are you the special one?"

"Me?" His gaze slid toward me. "I am not special. I'm no different than the rest."

"Not true," I said, as I shook my head. "You're like a legend in your own family. You're the one who defied your mother and married someone she didn't like—twice now—the entire neighborhood remembers you, Moroz said only the best would ever do for you—"

"All right, all right, I get it. But have you considered that everyone's only acting this way around me because I haven't been home in a few years?"

"That's a good point." We stopped at a light, and I watched as a small army of pedestrians crossed the street. "Why did it take you so long to come home again?"

"I told you, last time I was here it was a matchmaking disaster."

"But you don't let stuff like that bother you," I countered. "You are the most patient, easygoing person I've ever met, and you freely admitted that your family was only looking out for you. It's not like you to hold a grudge, especially not for this long."

"I don't know if I'd call it holding a grudge, but you're right. I deliberately stayed away." Dan blew out a breath. "I wasn't mad at anyone, except maybe myself. When I came home last time, my life was in shambles. I was a widower, I hadn't been to work in months, I was close to losing the house—"

"Really? I thought the house was paid for."

"It is now, but at the time, I didn't know Char had a life insurance policy. The settlement came the January after I was last home." Dan drummed his fingers on the steering wheel. "You know, the only person I talked to about the house was Nonna. You don't think she had anything to do with the settlement, do you?"

"I have never known a seer to influence a life insurance policy," I replied. "However, we tend to know a lot of powerful people, and she's probably accumulated a great deal of wealth over the centuries. She could have paid off your house herself, or sent you a check and documents to make it look like an insurance payout in order to save your pride."

"Proud? Me?" Dan flashed me a smile. "You're thinking of Frank Junior."

"Nah. I only think about you, baby," I said, paraphrasing him.

We laughed and joked until Dan pulled into Nonna's driveway. "No cars," I observed. "Is everyone at work?"

"Possibly," Dan said. "Although it's winter break, so Dad isn't teaching, and the girls don't work."

"What about your mom?"

"She doesn't have time to work, what with all she does around the house." Dan glanced at me. "I know. You're going to say we sound like a family of witches living off of our accumulated wealth."

"I was not going to say that." I would have called them a clan, rather than a family. "Let's see what our favorite nonna's up to."

We entered Nonna's level of the house through the side door. In the yard I saw the greenhouse I'd visited in my arsenic induced vision, but just like Dan said, it was closed down for the winter. Even so, I really wanted to have a look around in there and see what there was to see. Maybe there were some leftover belladonnas I could talk to.

"Nonna?" Dan called, as he cracked the door open. "Can Eli and I come in?"

"Of course," she called, then Nonna herself met us at the door wearing an apron over her housecoat and slippers. "Why you come this way? Avoiding the llama?" Nonna added, with a wink toward me.

"Llama?" Dan asked.

"Inside joke," I said. Dan took my coat and his, and went to hang both of them up. "Don't get me in trouble," I whispered to Nonna.

"Never, piccolina." Nonna put her hands on the sides of my face and looked into my eyes. "You feel good? The Acqua Tofana no hurt you?"

"I can handle a bit of arsenic," I said, and Nonna smiled. "All of these baneful herbs are throwing Dan for a loop, though."

Nonna patted my cheek. "Danny has Tofana blood. He strong."

"He is," I agreed. "Warn me about the poison next time?"

"Warning no fun." I followed Nonna into the kitchen, where pots of all shapes and sizes bubbled and steamed on the stove. "You eat yet?"

"We went to a diner for breakfast." I watched Nonna bustle around the stove for a few moments. "According to my father, you knew my grandmother."

"I know a lot of grandmothers. What her name?"

"Helena Moore."

Nonna stopped moving. "Knew? Helena gone?"

"She is."

"That too bad. Helena was a good girl. A bit of a stick in the mud, but a strong Matriarch." Nonna brought over some coffee and cookies. "No poison. Promise."

"I believe you. Did you not get along with my Gran?"

"It not that," Nonna replied. "Helena born here. She no grow up in the Old Country, and was shocked by our ways." Nonna glanced toward the ceiling. "If Helena knew I had a spirit trapped upstairs, she scream and cry until she figure out how to free him."

I'd never known Gran to scream or cry, but that was beside the point. "Are you ready to tell me why he's up there?"

"Depends. You scream at me?"

"Never." When Nonna only frowned, I said, "If you're not ready to talk about the guy upstairs, you can always tell me why everyone treats Dan like a king around here."

"Danny is a king," Nonna replied. "When Theresa born, I hope she take after my line, but no. She no sensitive, and neither were the next four children. But Danny, he is like me."

"Are you saying Dan's a seer?"

"No exactly," Nonna replied. "Family line is, come se dice, watered down by now. Many of the old families no as strong as they once were. Everyone come to America to start fresh, but no one stop to think what they lose."

"Is that what you did? Come here to start fresh?"

"Yes and no. You know who my mother was?"

"I do."

"Then you know why Italy no the best place for me. So I go to Greece, then I board a ship that bring me here, and here I stay." Nonna eyed me. "The Moores, they come here long ago, but they still strong."

"We do okay."

"More than ooo-kay," Nonna said, drawing out the syllables. "Danny need a strong seer like you, to help draw out his Tofana blood. Like calls to like, yes?"

"I-I guess."

Dan picked that moment to return to the kitchen. "I was saying hello to everyone upstairs," he explained, as he claimed the stool next to me. "Nonna, you won't poison me this time, will you?"

Nonna swatted the air near Dan to teach him a lesson, and returned to the stove. "No you worry, Danny. I only use poison to say hello to my new friend."

Dan turned to me and raised an eyebrow. "I told you, seers poison each other all the time," I said. "When I told my dad about the poison, he wasn't even fazed."

"I was fazed," Dan said. "Nonna, you've got to ease me into these things."

Nonna laughed, and brought him a cup of coffee and his own plate of cookies. "You both stay for lunch?"

"We can do that," Dan said. "We got Ma something, too, from up at Maple Acres."

"Maple Acres? Why you go see Moroz?"

"It was Eli's idea."

Nonna waggled her big wooden spoon at me. "Just like Helena. Already causing trouble."

Lunch in the dining room was... Well, the food was good.

Everyone was in attendance, including Dan's brothers, their spouses, and all the nieces and nephews, though the kids ate at their own special table in the kitchen. Dan's father, Frank Senior, sat at the head of the main table like a king in his castle, and Patty was seated on his left. At the opposite end of the table was Theresa; Dan explained that since she was the oldest child, she got the second best spot.

"You have a lot of family hierarchy," I whispered.

"Have to, when there's this many people," he whispered back.

I didn't argue with that, since I'd grown up as an only child. For all I knew, I was still an only child, even though my mother had some kids in her house in one of the false realities Dan and I had gotten stuck in. She'd refused to answer me when I asked if they were her kids, which was just typical for her. Regardless, I was new to sibling dynamics, so I decided to just go with the flow. At least the table was big enough for everyone.

As for Nonna, she bustled in and out of the dining room dropping off platters and bowls of food. Eventually she decided we had enough, and went into the kitchen to eat with the kids. I almost joined her.

For a little while, we all ate in peace. Then the interrogation started.

"So Danny," Carmelo, the oldest brother, began. He was on the police force, and had put in a good word for Dan back when he first applied to the academy. "How's work going?"

"Work is good," Dan replied. "Eli and I took on a bunch of new cases just before we left. We'll be pretty busy for the next few weeks."

"Cases?" Patty repeated, then she speared me with her gaze. "Are you also a police officer, Eliza?"

"Me? No," I replied. "I don't do well with authority. I own a detective agency."

Patty's laser gaze moved back to Dan. "It's not a conflict of interest for you to investigate these cases in your spare time?"

Dan put down his fork. "Ma. You know I left the force."

At that, the room went dead quiet. Frank Senior sat back in his chair and folded his hands across his stomach. "You left?"

I realized that was the first time I'd heard Dan's father speak. Even when we were introduced the other day, Frank Senior had only nodded toward me. Now that I heard his voice, and felt the chill that crawled down my spine, I understood why he didn't speak more often. His voice was layered in magic.

Dan glanced around the table. Everyone was watching him. "Are we doing this now?"

"It appears that we are," Frank Senior said.

"First of all, Ma knew all about this," Dan began. "I don't know why she didn't tell you. Second, I didn't leave so much as I got suspended and never went back."

"Eliza got you suspended?" Theresa demanded in her shrill voice. "Fricken' home wrecker!"

"Really?" I countered. "That the best you got?"

"Enough," Dan bellowed. "Eli had nothing to do with it. I hated being on the force from day one, and I finally left. And for the record, I don't know what problem you people have with my wife, but know that she's not going anywhere. You all can stick your opinions right up your asses for all I care."

The room went silent for a second time. I was a second away from suggesting Dan and I get out of there, when Frank Senior chuckled. "That's my Danny, never letting anyone push him around," he said, then he turned his gaze toward me. "Eli—may I call you Eli?"

"Of course," I said, too shocked by this about face to say anything else.

"Thank you. Eli, please let me take this moment to formally welcome you to the family. You make Danny very happy, and it's plain how much he loves you. Therefore, we love you too." Frank Senior smiled as big diamond like tears welled up in his eyes. "Welcome, daughter."

"Thank you," I whispered. Dan hooked his arm around my shoulders and kissed my cheek. "Thank you so much."

The rest of our meal went smoothly. Even Theresa and Dolores behaved, which was a Christmas miracle is there ever was one. While I appreciated the pleasant mood, I couldn't shake the fact that once Frank Senior had declared me a family member, everyone's attitude immediately changed about me. What's more, it wasn't his words that had made a difference, so much as what was behind them.

Frank Senior's voice had power. But where was it coming from?

After lunch, Dan and I helped Nonna clear the plates from the kids' table. I scraped while she rinsed, and Dan loaded the dishwasher. It was a pretty solid system.

"During lunch, I hear my Frank welcome you," Nonna said, when Dan went back to the table to collect more plates.

"He sure did," I said. "It was nice. I appreciate all you and your family have done for me."

Nonna patted my arm. "But you like Helena, so you want to know about his voice."

"Is it that obvious?"

"Helena was never sneaky, always very open about what she wanted. You same." Nonna pointed at the ceiling.

"What?" I asked. "Is there a cobweb?"

"The spirit," she said, and I could have smacked myself. Of course she meant the spirit. "I tell you it was no a good time for us to be in Italy, but I no tell you why."

"I thought it was because of the poisonings."

Nonna snorted. "There was no way they could catch me. Even if they did, I make sure they die in their sleep." She rinsed off a handful of forks and set them aside. "Do you believe in gods?"

"I do." I'd seen and heard enough in my life to know that even if actual gods didn't exist, there were some amazingly powerful beings in the world that had been treated as gods.

"Well, a few years after the chaos about the poison die down, I meet a man. Oh, Eliza, he was beautiful. Thick dark hair, full beard, and so, so muscular."

"Sounds like Dan," I said.

"Danny take after him, though he leave when the kids still babies," she said. "Older kids call him Grandpa Bo, but to me he always Boreas."

"Oh, like the north wind." When Nonna only stared at me, I set down the plate I was cleaning and faced her. "Wait. Your husband—my husband's ancestor—is the north wind?"

"Yes," she replied. "Frank inherit his voice."

"Yeah, he did," I murmured. "Why is he trapped upstairs?"

"Oh, Boreas no upstairs," Nonna said. "That my first husband, Enzo. He still love me, and no want to move on."

"How sweet," I murmured. "Are you still with Boreas?"

"We have no seen each other in many years," Nonna said. "He wind, can't be in one place. Me, I stay with the children, but we still together. Time apart is good for people like us."

"Enzo didn't mind you hanging around with Boreas?"

"Enzo was already dead."

"Then I guess his opinion didn't matter much," I said. "Dan can hear Enzo too, you know."

"Really?" Nonna didn't hide her surprise. "Since when?"

"The mark I gave Dan made him able to sense magic," I replied. "It's not how I intended the mark to work, but now that I know more about your family, I understand why it worked out the way it did."

"Rare for seer to give mark, unless trained," Nonna said. "You mention your father before. Little Alex, Helena's boy?"

"Yes," I said; my father had served as the seers' marksman since before I was born. "Gran only ever had one child. I'm an only child, too."

"Then you new Mistress of Seers."

"I was," I said softly. "I... I can't do it anymore."

"Piccolina," Nonna said, as she set her hand on my forearm, "we no always get to choose."

"I was Mistress, but something... Something happened." I squeezed my eyes shut as my mind replayed the images of me destroying Amir's soul. "I eliminated someone."

"Why? They bad?"

"Yeah," I said, as I snuffled. "He was bad. Very, very bad."

"That come with power," Nonna said. "Everyone look to us to lead, and to punish. No one stop to think what it cost us in the end."

I nodded, my throat too tight to speak. Dan returned with another stack of plates, and set them down hard when he saw us. "What happened?" he demanded.

"I was telling Nonna about what happened with Amir," I said, as I wiped my cheek with my shoulder.

"He got what was coming to him," Dan said, then he dabbed at my cheeks with a napkin. "You did what you had to do. It sucked, and you shouldn't have had to do it, but the world is better off without Amir in it."

"See that?" Nonna said. "My smart Danny, he understand."

"Dan is the literal best." I smiled at her, and then Dan, and for a few minutes we all quietly worked together.

As I scraped off the last plate, I asked, "What's up with the mistletoe man?" Dan stopped loading the dishwasher and gaped at me. "What?

We've got questions, and Nonna's got answers. Might as well ask her now."

Nonna shook her head. "Moroz bad news. Always has been."

"If he's bad news, why have we been going up to his farm all these years?" Dan countered.

Nonna frowned. "If you want to know why Patty go to Moroz, you need to ask Patty."

"Okay, I'll ask Ma." Dan finished loading the dishwasher, and set it to run. "What can I ask you about?"

"What you want to know?" Nonna countered.

"Everything," Dan replied. "But I'll settle for one thing."

"You, settle?" Nonna made a shooing motion with her hand. "Bah."

"Settle for now," he amended. "Why is it that I'm just now learning about all this magic that's been happening right here under my nose?"

"Simple," Nonna said. "You no interested in magic before, but Eliza bring your own magic to the surface. Like calls to like, and love make you gifts blossom."

Chapter Nine
The Bargain

After we finished up in the kitchen, Nonna went upstairs for a nap, then I went out to the car and grabbed the mistletoe and holly arrangement we'd picked up at Maple Acres. When I came back inside, I found Eli checking out Nonna's spice cabinet.

"Looking for poisons?" I asked, only half joking.

"They're all on the top shelf," Eli replied. "Probably so the kids can't reach them." She shut the cabinet door, and grimaced when she saw the arrangement. "You really want to ask your mother these questions now?"

"Like you said about Nonna, we've got questions and she's got answers." I started toward the stairs. "You with me?"

Eli laced her fingers with mine. "Always. Wait," she added, tugging me to a stop. "Nonna told me something I think you should know."

I mentally braced myself. "Tell me."

"You know how your father has that powerful voice," she began. "Nonna told me you're all descended from Boreas. You know, the North Wind. Your dad inherited his voice."

Boreas, if I recalled correctly, was a minor Greek god. "Is he the one screaming upstairs?"

"No. That's her first husband, Enzo."

I shut my eyes and took a breath. "Let's think on that later. Ma first, Nonna and her husbands second."

"Sounds good," Eli said, then she stood on her toes and kissed my cheek. "Let's do it."

I often wondered if Eli understood how much her support meant to me. Even before we'd been a couple—hell, before we'd even been friends—she always had my back, no matter the situation. Now she walked beside me as we went upstairs to confront my mother about whatever was going on with Mr. Moroz and his freaky mistletoe.

We found Ma in the upstairs kitchen, getting ready for dinner. I took one look at the bag of flour and the flat of eggs sitting on the counter and immediately knew what she was making. Eli made her best guess and was one hundred percent wrong.

"Is she making a cake?" Eli asked.

"Pasta," I replied. "Ma's fettuccini is legendary."

"You haven't had it in so long I'm surprised you remember," Ma said, as she emerged from the pantry with an armload of ingredients.

"I've never known anyone to make their own pasta," Eli said. "Is it hard?"

"Not really," Ma replied. "I can teach you how to make it."

"Really?" Eli asked, her eyes brightening. For someone who had grown up steeped in old-fashioned lore and ancient traditions, she loved learning new things. "It won't be too much trouble?"

"Of course not," Ma replied. "In fact, I'd love to teach you. None of my girls cook, you see."

"They don't need to, what with all the great food you and Nonna already make," Eli said.

Ma smiled. "That's very sweet of you. Go wash your hands, and we'll get started."

Eli did as asked, then Ma showed her how to make a well in the flour, the correct amount of eggs to add into that well, and how to mix it all up with a fork. Then they kneaded everything together, and made a hell of a mess in the process. Soon enough, the mess was contained, and they each had a ball of dough, though Eli's was looking a bit rough.

"I don't know if mine will be any good," Eli said, eyeing the difference between her uneven dough and Ma's perfect sphere.

"Nonsense," Ma said, as she covered both of the dough balls in plastic wrap and set them aside. "It will taste just fine. We need to let it rest for a while, then I'll show you how to roll it out and cut it. Unless you two have someplace else to be?"

"Actually, we have something for you," I said, then I took the holly and mistletoe arrangement out of the bag and set it on the counter. Ma took one look at it and melted.

"Oh, it's beautiful," she said. "Does this mean what I think it means?"

I glanced at Eli. She shrugged. "What exactly do you think this means?" I asked.

"That I'll have a new grandchild soon." Ma's gaze was fixated on the arrangement, so she didn't see Eli go white as a sheet. "I remember when your father and I were first married. We tried and tried for a baby, but nothing happened for the longest time. Then we went up to the farm and got this exact arrangement. Ten months later, our Theresa was here."

"Hmm." I fingered a deep green holly leaf. "Did you go to Maple Acres intending to get one of these?"

"Oh, no," Ma said. "We went there for a Christmas tree. But then we met Mr. Moroz, and he saw that we were childless, and suggested we take home one of these arrangements."

"Suggested?" Eli said. She'd regained her composure and was in full investigator mode. "Did Moroz imply that an arrangement such as this one could help you get pregnant?"

"Are you implying I was having problems getting pregnant?" Ma shot back.

"You yourself said you and Frank Senior tried for a while, with no results," Eli said. "That must have been hard."

"It was." Ma's throat worked, then she grabbed Eli's hand. "I don't want it to be hard for you two. Danny's got such a big heart, and I can see how much he loves you. He would love a baby just as much, maybe more."

"He would," Eli said. "I love him, too. But—and I'm not saying this to upset you in any way—we're not trying to get pregnant."

"You're not?" Ma's gaze shot from Eli to me. "Why not?"

"It's just not the time," I said. "We just got married. We need some time with just the two of us, before we can start thinking about adding more people into the mix."

"Time is a good thing," Eli said. "The more, the better."

Ma leaned closer to Eli, and said, "I understand. I was scared, too, but don't wait too long. The girls can't have babies until Danny does."

"What?" I demanded. "What does me having kids have to do with my sisters?"

Ma turned to me, and said, "That was the bargain we made with Mr. Moroz."

Two hours later, Eli knew how to roll out and cut pasta, Ma had told us all about how she made a deal with Moroz so she could have children, and I was convinced everyone in my family was nuts, myself included.

"Don't be too hard on Patty," Eli said, as we headed out to the truck. "Society puts a lot of pressure on women to be mothers, some cultures more than others. Women have done a lot crazier things than hang mistletoe in all their doorways in order to become parents."

"I guess you're right." I watched as Eli snapped a picture of the thermometer mounted next to the back door. It was set up to be visible to whoever was looking out the kitchen window. "What's that for?"

"Just a theory." We got into the truck, and Eli immediately turned on the heated seats. "I feel like an ice cube."

"It's not that bad." I turned around so I could back down the driveway, and saw some mistletoe scattered across the back seat. "Looks like some of those plants wanted to stay with us."

Eli twisted around in her seat so she could see the plants, and frowned. "Or Moroz enchanted them to stay with you."

"Think he could do that?"

"Clearly, he can do a lot more than just whip up some cold air and snow." She reached into the back, and grabbed a handful of the plants. "I have to say, now that we understand the bargain he struck with your mother, I get why all the decorations are mistletoe."

I grunted, and concentrated on driving. According to my mother, during her first visit to Maple Acres Farms, Moroz went on about the various medicinal properties of the plants in his shop. When he got to the fertility enhancing aspects of mistletoe and holly, Ma paid attention. Dad thought it was all bunk, but Ma went back a week later by herself and bought a flat of Moroz's fancy European mistletoe.

The real kicker is that, according to Moroz, since Ma gravitated to the mistletoe, all of her male children need to have at least one child before any of her daughters could have children of their own. At the time, grandchildren were so far in the future Ma didn't care one way or the other. Now, I was the last holdout.

I glanced at Eli. Actually, my wife was the last holdout.

"What's odd is that Moroz bothered with any of this," Eli continued. "You said your mother tried to get Charlotte to undertake some kind of fertility treatment. Think it was this?" Eli wiggled her handful of mistletoe at me.

"Char never said what specifically Ma wanted her to do," I replied. "However, nothing would have worked, magical or otherwise. Char had a hysterectomy before I ever met her." I glanced at Eli, and continued, "But if Ma had tried to insinuate that mistletoe or anything could magically induce pregnancy, Char would have told her to pound sand."

"Which she kind of did," Eli murmured. "Maybe that act irritated Moroz. Maybe he was expecting more kids by now, but you threw a wrench in his plans."

"Maybe." I glanced at Eli. She was weaving the plants into a wreath. "You sure you should be handling all of that?"

"I told you, it's a weak poison at best."

"I'm not worried about you getting poisoned. What about the fertility aspect?" It hurt my heart to ask that, but I knew Eli didn't want kids just yet. Hell, she'd just barely warmed up to the idea of maybe someday having them. The last thing she needed was a surprise baby.

But my girl, she wasn't worried or freaked out. She smiled, and said, "I'm a half witch seer, remember? We've got notoriously low birth rates. Always have."

"Not that low, since you're here." And thank God she was. I couldn't imagine my life without Eli. But her explanation made me recall another fact I'd recently learned. "Riddle me this. Wouldn't a god—or a powerful individual pretending he's a god—experience a similarly low birth rate?"

"You're referring to Boreas," she said, and I nodded. "I would think so. The issue of fertility is linked to life spans. Since supernaturals live so much longer than regular mortals, we don't need to reproduce as often. Yet here's the huge Lyons clan, reproducing like rabbits." Eli set the mistletoe down on the dashboard. "I know you've got all those nieces and nephews, but what about the rest of your family? Are there tons of aunts and uncles and cousins out there, too?"

"Not really," I replied. "I had some cousins out in Jersey, but they went to Scotland a while back. The family is really just what fits in Nonna's house."

"Interesting." Eli drummed her fingers on her leg.

"What's interesting?"

"In all the stories about gods and mortals getting together, there's one kid, maybe two, and that's it. Yet Boreas has an entire brood here in Queens. What if Moroz targeted your parents in order to have more of Boreas's descendants born in this area?"

"How would Moroz know who we're descended from?"

"Who knows? Maybe Moroz knew Boreas from way back. Maybe he was at Boreas and Nonna's wedding. But when we were at Maple Acres, Moroz said he would keep it winter year round if he could. I think he wants to use the cold north wind to do it."

"But we don't influence the wind," I began, then I remembered my father's voice. It had always been powerful, and whenever he gave a lecture, his students sat in rapt attention. "Dad's voice."

"Exactly. Your dad has an aspect of the god, and so do you."

"I do?"

"Your intuition, and Nonna says you look like Boreas."

"Wait. Are you saying I look like a god?"

"I take it back. But," she paused to tap the temperature display on the dashboard screen, "the area near your house is colder that the surrounding area. I noticed it the other day; I was freezing at Nonna's, but fine when we walked around the city. Remember how I took a picture of the thermometer on the back porch? It's five degrees colder at Nonna's than it is a few blocks away, which is significant."

"If all of this is significant, why doesn't it make any sense?" She'd mentioned gods, voices, and extra cold temperatures. None of that added up.

Eli took my hand in both of hers. "We'll figure out what's up. We always do."

Chapter Ten

Holly Is For Vengeance

Hours later, we were snuggled in our hotel bed and I was dreaming about endless stacks of fluffy, syrupy diner pancakes, and a parade of never empty coffee mugs. Then I was rudely awakened when Dan attacked my legs with his unkempt feet.

"Hey," I mumbled. "Stop scratching me." When the scrapes didn't subside, I pushed Dan's arm. "Quit it."

"Quit what?" he asked, his voice heavy with sleep. "I'm not even moving."

"Your feet are scratching me," I said as I opened my eyes and flung off the blankets. I expected to see Dan's toenails pressed against my shin. Instead, I saw a bed full of holly branches and their pointy, prickly leaves.

"Dan? Dan!" I stumbled out of bed, got tangled in the sheets, and ended up tripping and landing on my butt. "Dan, get up! The bed is full of holly!"

"Where did all these leaves come from?" Dan demanded, as he got out of bed and swept the holly leaves onto the floor. "I'm calling housekeeping."

"It's not housekeeping," I said, as I cowered on the rug. "It's Moroz."

"He is a fricken' asshole," Dan muttered. "How poisonous is this stuff? Some of the berries burst. Could we get sick?"

A vision of the smoke baby flitted behind my eyes and I remembered that while mistletoe affected a man's fertility, holly affected the woman. "I'm going to take a shower," I declared, and fled to the bathroom. I got in the shower and turned up the water as hot as it would go, and chanted every counterspell I knew. There was no way I would allow Moroz's icy magic to take hold of me, and I would not let this holly influence me or Dan to do anything, not if I could help it.

A few minutes later, Dan entered the bathroom. "Can I join you?"

"Yeah." I turned down the water's temperature, since Dan wasn't a fan of boiling himself alive like I was. He stepped into the tub, and pulled me into his arms.

"I bagged up all the holly and left it in the hall," he said, as the water flowed over my back. "Did the leaves scratch you up?"

"They did, but they didn't draw blood. I'm okay." I pressed my cheek against his chest as I clutched his hand and stared at the shower curtain; we had an agreement that we could tell each other anything while we were holding hands without fear or judgement. "I'm scared."

"Of Moroz?"

"No. Not him." I took a breath, and tried to organize my thoughts from the terrified jumble in my mind into something coherent. "I'm scared that I'll be a bad parent, like my mother was."

"Not possible," Dan said. "You're nothing like your mother. You're kind, and compassionate, and you put every other person in the world before yourself. Eliza, you will be a great parent, just like how Alex and Helena were great parents to you."

I nodded, but didn't let up my grip on his hand. "What if I manifested the holly?"

"Would you really do that? And, could you?"

"I've done it before," I replied. "I didn't mean to manifest all those acres of bleeding hearts when we were first together, but I did. Tessa thinks I manifest baneful herbs all the time. All that holly in the bed could have been from me."

"Let's say you did create it. What does it mean?"

"Self-fulfilling prophecy? The girl with the awful mother grows up and becomes an even worse mother." I snuffled, and hid my face against Dan's chest. While it was no secret that I'd never wanted kids, I'd never told anyone exactly why I didn't want them. Dan, being the kind man he was, accepted my reluctance and never questioned my forced childless state too deeply. But I'd never woken up in a bed full of holly before, and now all my fears were coming to the surface.

Now he knew that it wasn't so much that I didn't want kids. I worried that some part of me was like my mother, and I never wanted anyone to be treated the way she'd treated me.

"First of all, that won't happen," Dan said. "Second, would you really create a bushel of holly to prove that? The bleeding hearts had context. Holly appearing out of nowhere doesn't seem the same."

"It is weird," I said. "Before we were at Maple Acres, I'd never really thought of holly in conjunction with fertility, either. There's lots of other plants I would have thought of, but not holly."

"When you do think about holly, what comes to mind?"

"You can banish unwanted spirits with a holly wand," I began, then I recalled another use. "Vengeance. Holly can help the bearer exact revenge."

"Then the question is, who wants revenge?" Dan worked his fingers into my wet hair. "Do you want revenge against someone?"

"I'm not into revenge." I'd been known to hold an epic grudge or two, but my version of getting even was to live a happy life with as few jerks in it as possible. "And if I did choose vengeance, I'd go about it quickly and quietly. Flashy holly branches aren't my style."

"What is your style?" Dan asked. "Belladonna and black coffee?" We laughed, and for a moment it was just me and Dan and the water, and life was perfect. "So, you don't think someone who's not currently in this bathroom is trying to make you, I don't know, extra fertile?"

"Why would anyone do that?" I countered. "The only person that wants me to get pregnant is you. Though, I guess your mom wants another grandkid, too." Dan's brow pinched, and I wanted to kick myself. "I'm sorry, that came off harsher than I intended."

"I'll forgive you, but only because you were woken up by a bunch of prickly leaves," he said. "And it's not just Ma and me. Moroz is apparently invested in Ma getting a bunch of grandchildren."

"But, why?" I mumbled, feeling foolish because here I was freaking out over myself, but these were plans Moroz had set into motion decades ago. I needed to pay attention to the details, and not get swept up in my own emotions. "What could he possibly want with all these kids? Is he building an army?"

"No idea, but why are my sisters in limbo until I have a kid?" Dan shook his head. "It doesn't make any sense."

"We're definitely missing something, and I'm all set with this shower." I turned off the water, then I stepped out of the tub and began blotting my hair. Dan grabbed a second towel, and started drying my back. "Thank you, for putting up with me."

"If anything, you're putting up with me." Dan wrapped the towel around my waist, then he lifted me in his arms.

"I can walk, you know," I reminded him.

"I know you can," he said, then he carried me back to bed. Since I loved it when he held me, I didn't complain. He paused when we reached it, and asked, "Should we sleep here, or did the holly contaminate it? I can call down for new sheets, or we could change rooms."

"I don't want to bother the staff. With the leaves gone, it should be fine." Dan sat on the bed, keeping me in his arms. "Is Moroz always at the farm?"

"He's been there every time I've been up there," he replied. "Why?"

"I want to go there when he's not on site. I want to have a thorough look around, and talk to the plants." I moved so I could look Dan in the eye. "Whatever his true plan is, I think it's hurting your family. We need to figure out what he's up to, and undo it, if we can."

Dan searched my face, then he leaned over and grabbed his phone. "If we leave now, we'll get there just after midnight," he said, as he checked the screen. "One, at the latest."

"You want to go now?"

"If whatever he's up to is affecting my family, yes. Let's get moving, and stop him as fast as we can."

Chapter Eleven
Ded Moroz

While Dan and I got dressed, and I blow dried my hair, we discussed the best and worst ways to get into Maple Acres for some reconnaissance. We soon realized that if we were going to be sneaky, we would need to arrive in a vehicle that Moroz hadn't seen before, and wasn't registered to Dan. Since all the legit rental places were closed at that time of night, Dan called his friend Andreas, also known as Mama Anastasia's son, and asked to borrow his car. And that was why we were driving toward Astoria in the dead of night.

"Andreas is really all right with this?" I asked Dan. We were on our way to Andreas's place, where we would trade our truck for his and then drive out to Maple Acres. "He doesn't even know where we're taking his car."

"Doesn't matter," Dan replied. "Andreas is to me like Tessa is to you. We've got each other's backs, no matter the situation. And he's practically family. Remember when I told you about Alicia's sole long-term relationship, the one that fizzled out? It was with him."

"Oh, wow. Was that awkward, having your friend and sister be together like that?"

"You know, it wasn't. It was actually nice, and they treated each other really well."

"Then why aren't they together now?"

"Neither one of them can explain why it never worked out. They just drifted apart." Dan turned onto a side street. "And, we're here."

Dan parked on the street in front of a brick house with a matching brick and wrought iron fence. The garage door was already open, probably because Andreas was waiting for us. I followed Dan into the garage, and saw a brand new Cadillac SUV idling away. It was the blackest car I'd ever seen, from the body paint, to the wheels, to the darkly tinted windows.

Standing next to the truck was a man who was the opposite of darkness in every way. He was tall and broad shouldered, with golden hair and sparkling blue eyes. And he was looking at Dan like he'd finally reunited with his long-lost brother.

"Andreas," Dan said, then they hugged like old friends. "Thank you for lending us your truck."

"Any time, Danny," Andreas replied. "Is this your Eliza?"

"Sure is," Dan replied. I stepped forward and waved. Andreas looked me over, and nodded.

"It's good to meet you, Eliza," Andreas said. "Mama was quite impressed with you when you stopped by for breakfast. She said you have a good heart, and I can see that to be true."

"Thank you," I said. Normally, that sort of talk would raise my hackles, but I'd been pondering Mama Anastasia ever since we met at the diner. There was something magical and otherworldly about her, not unlike Nonna. It was only natural that those qualities extended to her son. "I really appreciate your help tonight."

"Think nothing of it. And I have something else for you." Andreas handed us two black hooded sweatshirts. "I got these from my father. You could say he's pretty good about not being seen when he doesn't want to be. Put these on when you're at the farm, and no one will recognize you. Even if surveillance footage captures you, the images will be blurry."

I accepted the sweatshirt, and felt the crackle of magic. Dan did too, based on his grin.

"What's in this?" Dan asked. "Magic threads?"

"Look at you, finally ready to see what's all around you," Andreas replied. "Take care of him, Eliza."

"Oh, I will," I replied. "This one's so innocent, he's like a babe in the woods."

"All right, all right," Dan said. "We've got places to be. I'll call you when we're on our way back."

"Sounds good," Andreas said, and he handed Dan the keys. "Don't do anything I wouldn't do."

Dan scoffed, then we got in the Cadillac. As Dan backed out of the garage and onto the street, I checked out the sweatshirts. They were solid black, had no tags or labels, and smelled like cypress.

"Exactly how much magic is going on out here in Queens?" I asked.

"This truck is nice, but I wouldn't call it magical."

"Not the truck, these magical sweatshirts. Your childhood bestie just handed us the modern equivalent of cloaks of invisibility."

Dan glanced at the sweatshirts in my lap. "Babe. You're reading into it."

"His mother runs a magical diner."

"He runs it too, now," Dan said. "Andreas is the head chef."

"Wait. Andreas made those glorious pancakes?" I twisted around in my seat and gazed out the back window toward Andreas's house. "Is he single?"

"Hey!"

"I'm just kidding." I faced forward, and resumed my examination of the sweatshirts. "Besides all of Andreas and his mother's magic, there's everything happening in Nonna's house. There's a lot going on out here."

"You do have a point," he allowed. "I guess the next step is to figure out how deep Moroz is in all this."

"I'll ask Tess if she knows anything about him," I said, since she knew all the supernatural gossip. "Maybe she'll have some insight."

"Or warnings," Dan added. I laughed, then I took out my phone, and started typing.

Eli: In today's episode of Eli's Mis-Adventures, she and Dan head out to Maple Acres to find out what's up with Ded Moroz.

I hadn't expected an immediate reply from Tess, but her response appeared less than a minute later.

Tessa: Be careful. The world paints him as a kindly Father Christmas figure now, but many of us remember when he was a demon called Morozko.
Eli: What was Morozko's deal?
Tessa: He delighted in freezing entire villages to death, until he accidentally froze the house his daughter was sleeping in. He's been searching for a replacement for her ever since.

"Dan," I began, then I relayed what Tessa had shared about Morozko. "We are rapidly getting in way over our heads."

"Seems that way," he said, not that he made any move to slow down or otherwise alter our plans. Dan was fearless when it came to protecting his family. "So, how are we going to handle this?"

"I don't think our core mission has changed. Not yet, anyway. After I talk to the plants, who knows?" I watched the dark roads speed by for a few minutes. "If Moroz is searching for a replacement daughter, do you think he wants one of your sisters?"

"That is a possibility," Dan allowed. "But why is he keeping them childless?"

"Maybe he doesn't want grandkids? Or maybe he wants a girl that doesn't grow up."

"That is a whole new level of disturbing."

"The more I learn about him, the worse he gets." I thumbed through some of the information Tess had emailed me. It was several accounts of Morozko getting offended at small or sometimes imagined affronts, and committing mass murder via ice storms as a result. The only person that had ever softened his murderous tendencies was his daughter. She would plead with him to spare lives and homes, and try to make him into a better man. All she got for her efforts was an icy death.

"Nonna was right," I said. "Moroz is bad news. Vain, capricious, below freezing bad news."

"Like the Abominable Snowman gone bad?" Dan asked. "Or Jack Frost with a grudge?"

"Sort of," I said, remembering all the holly in our bed. "But who's he mad at?"

We drove under the wooden arch and into Maple Acres' parking lot around three in the morning. Since it was the dead of winter, sunrise was still several hours in the future. That was good, since we needed all the darkness we could get to pull off this caper.

I handed Dan one of the sweatshirts we'd gotten from Andreas, then I pulled mine over my head. As my arms moved into the sleeves, I felt a crackle like static electricity, and a layer of energy settled onto my skin.

"Wow." I flipped down the visor and looked in the mirror. I was still recognizable, but I believed Andreas's claim that neither eyes nor surveillance cameras would be able to recognize us. "Your buddy knows his spell work. Do you think Andreas made my pancakes with actual magic?"

"All right. No more diner for you." When I gasped, he continued, "I don't need the competition."

I leaned over the center console and kissed him. "You have no competition," I said, and I meant it. Dan was endgame for me.

Dan cupped my cheek. "Neither do you, baby. We're in this together 'til the end."

"That's right we are." I set my hand on his stubbly cheek; I loved it when he didn't shave for a few days, and his whiskers were just beginning to soften. "Come on. Let's talk to the trees and see what's really going on here."

We got out of the Cadillac, and I immediately noticed the lack of a biting wind. "Notice how not frigid it is?" I asked. "This is regular cold weather, unlike last time we were here. That was 'oh my god, my nose is going to freeze off' cold weather."

"I can't sense any magic, either, except for what we brought with us," Dan said. "Working theory is that Moroz can only control his immediate surroundings."

"Agreed." I thrust my hands into my sweatshirt's front pocket, and briefly wondered if the magic that obscured our appearances was also keeping us warm... But if I mentioned that to Dan, would he freak out? "You didn't think I was serious when I asked if Andreas was single, did you?"

Dan looped his arm around my shoulders, and kissed my hair. "I know you weren't. I was just teasing you, baby."

"Good." We stood together for a moment, and I considered our next move. "Do we want to break into the store, or sneak around the forest?"

"The store would probably be warmer," Dan said. "I don't think wandering around a forest in the cold, dark night is our best option. There's a greenhouse behind the place, too. We missed it last time, but you'd probably like it in there."

"You've convinced me. Let's do the greenhouse," I said; those plants would probably be the healthiest, since they were still growing and hadn't been harvested. Healthy plants were more likely to have information to share, too. "Lead the way."

We kept our heads down as we crept past the front of the store. I didn't see any cameras, but that didn't mean they weren't there. In fact, I was willing to bet Moroz used every magical and mundane surveillance system he could get his icy cold hands on. That meant whatever he was protecting was special, and possibly powerful.

The greenhouse's entrance was a plain glass door, which was locked. Lucky for us, I had my lock picks on me, and we were inside in no time.

"Have I ever told you that you'd make a great criminal?" Dan asked.

"As my accomplice, you would know." I took a deep breath of the warm, humid air inside the greenhouse, and wondered yet again why I lived in New England. Maybe I could convince Dan to move somewhere that was warm year round, although that would put him even farther away from his family, who were firmly rooted in Queens.

"Why'd your cousins go to Scotland?" I asked, since they seemed to be the only ones in his family who had ever left the northeast. "And what's the weather like there?"

"The older one got into some legal trouble, so him and his sister went overseas to hide out until everything blew over," Dan replied. "Now they live in Glasgow. I can ask what the weather's like next time I talk to them."

"Do you talk to them often?"

"Not really. Just the odd birthday text, stuff like that. Why? You looking to move?"

"Just wondering what it would be like to live somewhere warm."

"Something tells me Scotland's not a tropical paradise," Dan said, then he found the light switch and flipped it on. After a bit of blinking, my eyes adjusted, and I got a look at the heart of Moroz's operation. Inside the greenhouse were dozens of potted broadleaf trees. Each one of trees was between three and four feet tall, and they all had a robust mistletoe specimen nestled in their branches.

"Weird," Dan said, as he approached one of the trees for a closer look. "These plants don't grow in their own dirt?"

"Mistletoe is a parasite. They siphon nutrients from their hosts, which in this case are these trees." I walked up and down the rows, and verified that each mistletoe specimen was the rarer European variety. What's more, based on the labels on the planters, all of these plants were clones. If these were clones, that meant there was a parent plant around here somewhere, and for Moroz to have expended this much effort on cloning, that parent must be awfully special.

"Where is the original plant," I muttered, as much to myself as the trees and their parasites.

"Babe," Dan said, as he pointed toward the far side of the room. "Is that golden glow like the one you saw at Nonna's?"

I turned around, and saw a golden light emanating from behind a room divider. I found that odd, because why would you want to divide one set of plants from the next? They were all the same variety, therefore cross pollination wasn't an issue.

Curious, I approached the light. Dan was behind me, telling me to be careful, but I ignored him. The light wouldn't hurt me. The light wanted to talk, to show me things. I wanted to listen, and learn.

Behind the divider, I found an exceptionally old grouping of mistletoe; the parent I'd been searching for. It wasn't attached to a tree, which was odd. Instead, it was sitting in a wide, shallow bowl, and I could see liquid reflecting beneath it. I reached out to touch one of the shiny, satiny green leaves, and images flooded my brain.

Ice

Anger

Pain

NO!

Everything went white, then black.

Chapter Twelve
Escape and an Alibi

No sooner had Eli touched the glowing mistletoe than she fainted dead away.

I reached out and grabbed her before she hit the floor. I almost didn't catch her. The force of her fall took both of us down to the concrete.

"Eli," I said to her, half frantic. "Eliza!"

She made a noise and moved her head. It wasn't a lot, but it was enough to reassure me that she was still alive. I stood with her in my arms, intending to get the hell out of there, when she grabbed my shoulder.

"The mistletoe," she rasped, as her fingers dug into me with more strength than a barely conscious person should have. "It doesn't want to be here."

"Okay. What can we do about that?"

"Grab it," she replied. "It needs to come with us."

I spun around and checked out the mistletoe. The plant in question was sitting in some kind of liquid, and my arms were already full of Eli. I looked around the room, and saw a stack of empty plastic pots in the corner. I set Eli down against the wall, then I grabbed one of the pots and set on the ground next to the mistletoe. My next move was to take the plant out of the bowl it was floating in, and let the liquid drip off it.

"That is not water," I said, as the thick, syrupy drops took their time slithering down off the roots and to the floor.

"It's blood," Eli whispered. "It hates the blood."

I tasted bile in the back of my throat. I'd never been squeamish, but parasitic plants floating in pools of blood were gross in an entirely unexpected way. I gave the plant a final shake, then I stuffed it in the empty pot. After I took a last look at our surroundings, and made sure we were still alone, I set the pot in the crook of Eli's arm, picked her up and carried her out of that greenhouse of horrors.

When we got outside, I was happy to learn that the air temperature remained cold but not frigid. I started toward the parking lot, when I noticed movement near the truck.

Moroz was looking into the truck's side window, and, based on his body language, he was pissed.

I backed behind the tree line. Once we had some cover, I leaned against the trunk of a pine, and assessed our options. They weren't good.

For one thing, we couldn't stay out here for long. The sun wasn't up and it was below freezing. That was a recipe for hypothermia if I ever heard one. Even if we did survive the next couple of hours outdoors, once the sun rose, it wouldn't be hard to spot Eli and me hiding among the trees, or getting into the truck. That meant we needed to get out of here under cover of darkness and as soon as possible. What we needed was a distraction, and a hell of a lot of luck.

Since my wife was a powerful witch, we didn't need luck. I just needed her to wake up for a few minutes.

"Eliza," I whispered, as I stroked her hair back from her face. "Eli, baby, I need you."

"I'm here," she mumbled. "What can I do?"

"We need to get to the truck, but Moroz is there," I began. "We need to draw his attention inside the shop so we can get out of here."

Eli nodded, then she set her hand on the mistletoe. "Tell your children to scream," she said. I didn't hear anything, but all of a sudden, Moroz ran inside the shop as if his life depended on it. While the coast was clear, I ran to the truck, got Eli and the blood-soaked plant in the back, then I jumped in the driver's seat and tore out of the parking lot like a bat out of hell.

"Where are we going?" Eli asked, after we'd been driving for around twenty minutes. She was sitting up, and had noticed the road signs I was speeding past.

"I'm going north for a bit," I replied. "That way, if Moroz sends anyone after us, we can lose them before we go back to the city."

"The truck's magic is pretty solid." Eli clambered over the seat like an acrobat, then she belted herself in and faced me. "I don't think anyone could follow us."

"Good." I reached over, and grabbed her hand. "You're okay?"

"I am." She kissed the back of my hand. "I didn't mean to scare you."

I resisted the urge to stop the car, pull Eli into my arms, and tell her how much she meant to me. We needed to get back to the hotel first, and then I'd accomplish those last two things. "Why did we take the mistletoe?"

"It saw Moroz kill his daughter," Eli replied. "And it doesn't think it was an accident."

"Really? Why is the plant still working with him?"

"It doesn't want to. Dan, Moroz has been holding this mistletoe hostage for years, taking clones and giving them to families all up and down the east coast."

"What's his game?"

"He wants a new daughter, just like we thought, but he also wants revenge."

When we got back to Andreas's place, he was waiting for us in the garage even though I'd forgotten to call him once we were on our way back. That made me wonder if the truck had some kind of magic alert system that let him know when we were close. Since there was no reason not to, Eli and I told him everything that went down at Maple Acres, right down to the lack of magic in the parking lot and Moroz peeking inside the truck. Andreas didn't say a word until we were done, though his attention was fixed on our rescued mistletoe the entire time.

"How old is this plant?" he asked, after we'd told him everything. I hadn't noticed it earlier, but the mistletoe had the same glass flower attached to it that decorated all of the finished arrangements. Moroz really liked marking his work. Reminded me of a serial killer.

"Decades," Eli replied. "It was there when Moroz killed his daughter."

"And the plant claims he froze her on purpose," Andreas said. "Do we know why Moroz did such a heinous thing?"

Eli shook her head. "I haven't figured it out yet. The mistletoe communicates in images rather than words, but they're hard to understand."

Andreas ran his hand over the crest of leaves. "Then this mistletoe is our only witness to the crime. We must keep it safe. Although, I don't have any soil to put it in."

"It doesn't need soil. It needs to attach to a tree," Eli said. "Broadleaf, preferably."

"There's a potted fig in the sunroom," Andreas said. "Will that do?"

Eli shrugged. "I'm not really sure, but we've got to work with what we've got."

"Here. Let me take it. I'll get it set up with the fig." Andreas took the plant, pot and all, and moved toward the stairs.

"I guess we'll get going," I said. It was near six in the morning, and after driving all night, sneaking around Maple Acres, and rescuing Eli and a random plant, I was beat.

"Actually, I think you two should stay here for the day," Andreas said. "While the Cadillac and the sweatshirts obscured your identity, Moroz knows you were interested in his mistletoe, and now his prized specimen is gone. If he comes looking for you, you'll need an alibi."

"And our alibi will be that we were here?" I asked.

"You pulled up around ten last night, and your truck hasn't moved since then. The security cameras have been trained on it the entire time. Also, the cameras didn't pick up the Cadillac entering or leaving the garage."

"Nice," Eli said. "What kind of wards are in place?"

"My mother's wards are the strongest in New York," Andreas replied; I guessed we were past pretending there was no magic happening. That was good. I liked transparency. "Moroz would need a literal army in order to breach them. He may be an old and powerful demon, but we have more than enough power of our own."

Eli nodded. If she approved of this arrangement, so did I. "Looks like we're having a sleepover," she said. "Are we taking the couch?"

"What kind of a host do you think I am?" Andreas asked, as he opened the door that led into the house. "Dan, you remember the downstairs apartment?"

"Do I ever." We'd spent so much time in that apartment as kids it was like my second home.

"Take your bride there, and get some rest. I'll make sure our other guest comfortable in the sunroom. If you need anything, call me."

Andreas headed toward the sunroom on the south side of the house. I took Eli's hand, and led her down to the apartment. "Is every house in Queens a split level ranch, like your gran's place?" she asked.

"This isn't really a split level," I said. "The apartment is more of an oasis."

"Oasis? Like water in the desert?"

"Come on. You'll see."

I opened the door and flipped on the light, and heard Eli gasp. "Holy fricken' shit!"

Chapter Thirteen
The Oasis

When Dan called this place an oasis, he wasn't kidding.

The floors were covered with warm terracotta tile, and the walls were painted in bright frescoes depicting olive groves and sunny meadows. The frescoes were bordered with wide stripes of gold leaf that perfectly matched the shiny wall sconces. Fluted marble columns stood in the corners, and the perimeter of the room was wrapped in a low sofa. In the center of everything was a round table, on top of which was a bowl of fruit.

"There's fresh fruit sitting out?" I picked up one of the three bright red pomegranates, mostly just to see if it was real. It was, and the rind was firm and unblemished. "Does someone live down here?"

"Nah. Andreas and his parents live upstairs."

"Then why is there a bowl of fruit on the table?" I picked up a banana. It was also real, and perfectly ripe. "Who leaves out piles of fresh fruit in an apartment they don't stay in?"

Dan shrugged. "As far back as I can remember, there's always been food down here. I bet the fridge is stocked, too." I followed Dan into the kitchen. The terracotta floor extended into there, and the counters and backsplash were covered with blue and white mosaic tiles. Dan opened the huge stainless steel fridge, and revealed shelves packed with sliced sandwich meat, cheeses, heaps of fresh vegetables, and even more fruit. This apartment that no one lived in had more food in it than Dan and I could eat in a week. I started opening cabinets. Each one was filled with canned and jarred goods.

"This is weird," I said, then I turned around and spied a porcelain cornucopia sitting on the counter. "Dan. Who are these people?"

"They're my friend Andreas, and his parents," Dan replied. "His dad is some sort of Greek millionaire. I never knew his exact business."

"I bet." I picked up the cornucopia, and willed it to tell me its secrets. Unlike the mistletoe, it stayed quiet. "You're sure we can trust them?"

"Absolutely." He took the cornucopia out of my hands and set it on the counter, then he wrapped his arms around me and tucked my head underneath his chin. "I've known Andreas since middle school. He's always had my back. And Mama Anastasia is one of the kindest people I've ever met."

I nodded against his shoulder. "I'm sorry. I don't mean to question your friends. If you trust them, I trust them."

"It's okay, baby." He pushed back my hair and kissed my forehead. "You're just being cautious. I get it." Dan glanced around the kitchen. "I guess this set up is a little unusual."

"Thank you, for humoring my theory," I said, then I yawned. "I take it there's a bedroom somewhere down here?"

Another kiss on my forehead. "This way."

Dan led me down the hall, and into what had to be the main bedroom. If the front of the apartment was decorated in a Mediter-ranean theme, the bedroom was full on Grecian splendor. The bed was made with pristine white sheets and a thick down comforter, and the headboard was draped with sheer blue netting that hung from a fixture on the ceiling. The walls and ceiling were painted sky blue and edged in gold, which was a bright yet soothing combination. There was a large closet on one side of the room, and the other had a set of doors that I was betting opened out to the garden. Between the two walls was a door that led to the bathroom.

"Can we live here?" I asked. Dan laughed, as if I wasn't as serious as I've ever been.

"Now you understand why I call it the oasis," he said, then he sat on the bed and pulled off his shoes. "I don't know about you, but I could sleep for a week."

"Same," I began, then I looked toward the bathroom. Something about the pedestal sink and blue and white tile floor was beckoning me in a profound way.

"I'm going to take a shower," I announced. "Wash off the magic, and all."

"Does magic need to be washed off?"

"Well, no. But Moroz has some weird shit going on, and we don't know whose blood the mistletoe was floating in. I think a shower's in order."

Dan made a face. "I'd like to never think about that bowl of blood ever again. While you do that, I'll put together something for us to eat."

"Sounds like a plan," I said, then I entered the bathroom and flipped on the light.

And entered heaven.

The entire bottom floor apartment was a thing of opulence and beauty, but this bathroom was on a whole different level. It was huge, easily as large as the front room, and was wrapped in white and rose gold tile. The back wall was taken up by an enormous soaking tub that was framed by stained glass windows—which were hopefully opaque during the day—and teak shelving that held dozens of glass bottles. Normally I would have made a beeline toward the tub, but I was too exhausted to spend an hour soaking. That was why I investigated the shower.

The shower, which was separate from the tub, was a walk in affair framed with clear glass. The walls were sparkling white subway tiles bordered with a blue and green mosaic, and the floor was a pebbled texture that I was certain would feel great on my bare feet.

I turned on the spray, and while the water warmed up, I took off my clothes left them in a badly folded pile on the counter. By the time that was done, the shower was nice and steamy, so I pulled open the glass door and stepped inside.

Heaven.

Dan and I showered together often, and the two we had at home were more than big enough for us; well, that's not quite true. The upstairs shower was definitely on the small side, but that was okay. We liked bumping up against each other. This one, however, could have fit me and five of my closest friends with room to spare. All this space, coupled with the sprig of eucalyptus hanging from above and more showerheads than any one person could possibly need, meant this shower put the average spa to shame.

The tiled ledge held an assortment of shampoos and body washes, because of course it did. I picked the body wash that looked the most moisturizing, and lathered away. As the bubbles rinsed off my skin and down the drain, I willed them to take any lingering essence of Moroz with them.

As amazing as the shower was, I didn't stay in it for too long. After I got out, I wrapped one fluffy white towel around my waist and used a second to blot my hair, then I joined Dan in the bedroom. He was sitting on the bed next to a huge platter of food.

"What's all this?" I asked, as I draped my hair towel around my shoulders.

"I'm starving, and I figured you were, too." Dan glanced up at me, and gave me the widest, goofiest grin.

"What?" I asked, as I looked in the mirror over the dresser. "Is something on me?"

"Nah. You're just gorgeous."

"Gorgeous?" I scoffed. "If anything, I look like a drowned rat."

He shook his head. "I love how you look when you first get out of the shower, with your hair all wet and your cheeks bright pink. Only I get to see you this way. It's special, you know?"

"Well, when you put it that way." I sat next to him, and kissed him. "I guess I have to agree."

"The fact that you're topless doesn't hurt, either."

I laughed against his lips. "The truth comes out."

"Always." Dan kissed me again, then he drew back and indicated the food. "I didn't know what you were in the mood for, so I brought some of everything."

After another peck, I checked out the platter. There was a big bowl of hummus surrounded by pita chips, carrots, olives, crackers, and a few types of cheese. Dan had also added a bunch of grapes and split open one of the pomegranates. Nestled amid everything was a jar of honey.

"Why did you bring out the honey?" I asked. "Please don't tell me you're going to dip carrots in there."

He picked up the jar, and looked at it instead of me when he replied. "When I saw this in the cupboard, all I could think about was licking it off you. Is that something you might want to do?"

"Yeah, why not." We'd never been shy with each other, especially not when it came to sex, but this was the first time he mentioned bringing food into the bedroom. "Do you like playing with food? Is that, um, something you've done with... before?"

"I've never once wanted to fuck with food, so to speak," he said, then he met my gaze. "But sometimes I do think about licking you."

"Oh." His admission sent a frisson of anticipation down my spine, and I felt the tips of my breasts tighten. "I like licking you, too."

We stared at each other for a moment, then we burst out laughing. "This has got to be the strangest conversation we've ever had, and we've had some doozys," Dan said, as he wiped tears from his eyes. "Do me a favor, babe, and put the food on the dresser?"

"Um, sure." I stood, and set the platter aside. "Why?"

Instead of answering me, Dan pulled the towel off my shoulders, then he grabbed my waist and tossed me onto the bed. My other towel fell off mid-toss, then Dan was standing over me with the jar of honey in his hand.

"Let's find out how sweet you really are."

Chapter Fourteen
Honey and the Truth

After Dan confessed his desire to play with honey and threw me on the bed, I lay there completely naked, while he loomed over me like an erotic mountain. One of his hands snaked up my inner thigh, while the other clutched the jar of honey like it was some sort of sexual weapon he meant to use against me.

Actually, he meant to conquer me. We would just see about that.

"Wait," I said, with a hand on his chest. Dan immediately stopped moving. He was serious when it came to consent, which never failed to arouse me further. "This isn't fair."

He blinked. "How so?"

"I want you naked."

His grin returned, and he set the honey aside. "Anything you want, baby," he said, as he pulled his shirt over his head. I took a moment to appreciate his strong arms, the smooth planes of his abdomen and well-muscled chest; Dan loved working out, and I loved the results. Then he pushed down his pants and his cock sprung free, and I forgot how to think. And breathe.

While I stared at Dan's erection, he got back on the bed and spread my legs farther apart. "And now, sweetness," he began, then he dipped his finger in the honey—I hadn't even seen him grab the jar again—and let it drip onto my breasts. "How's that feel?"

"Weird." I giggled at the absurdity of what we were doing. "I thought it would be cold, but it's warm. Kind of nice."

"Yeah? How about this," he said, as he closed his mouth over my breast. A sound escaped my lips that at any other time would have thoroughly embarrassed me. Right then, I just wanted Dan to keep touching me.

Finished with my breast, he drizzled honey down my abdomen and followed the sticky path with his mouth. "What about you?" I asked.

"What about me?" With two fingers, he scooped honey from the jar and spread it on my thighs. Electric shocks shot across my body, then Dan dragged his tongue across my entrance, and I forgot everything except the sensation of his hot, wet skin against mine.

Holy hell.

He went at me like a man possessed, licking and sucking my most sensitive skin while his hands gripped my hips. I cried out when I came, my orgasm having shattered me to pieces. I was still floating back to earth when he slid his cock inside me.

"I knew it," he said, between thrusts. "Sweetest thing in the world is your body. Fucking sweetest thing ever."

I grabbed onto the headboard as Dan's hips pistoned against mine. He was relentless, and it wasn't long before I came again. A moment later, Dan cried out and collapsed onto me, panting, his body slick with sweat.

"Eliza," he murmured, as he kissed my throat. "Eliza, baby. I love you. I love you so fucking much."

I kissed his sweaty, sticky with honey forehead. "I love you, too."

I lost track of how many times we had sex that morning. I definitely had no idea how many times I came. What I did know was that the bed was a mess, I might never walk again, and the jar of honey was almost empty. Interestingly enough, even though we hadn't slept, I wasn't the least bit tired.

"The honey turned out to be a good idea," I said, and Dan chuckled. He was laying on his back with one arm behind his head, and the other wrapped around my shoulders. My cheek was pressed against his chest, while I ran my fingers through the dark, soft hair on his abdomen. "We need to do some laundry. Is there a washer down here?"

"Probably," Dan said. "If not, we can use the one upstairs, or we can hit up the laundromat."

"The laundromat, huh? You take me to all the best places."

He kissed my hair. "You know it, baby." We were quiet for a few moments, then he asked, "Can I ask you about the greenhouse?"

I stilled, my fingers frozen mid-caress. "What about it?"

"When you passed out, you gave me the fright of my life," he said quietly. "You were fine, then you touched the mistletoe and dropped like a stone."

"My foresight's made me pass out before," I began, but Dan wasn't about to let me downplay what had happened.

"This was different," he said. "The other times were scary, yeah. This time, I didn't know if you'd wake up."

"You're right. This time was different." I wrapped my arm around his chest, seeking the warmth and safety only Dan could give me. "It scared me too, but not until later. Does that make sense?"

"Yeah. It does."

"I mean, I touch plants all the time. They're just leaves and flowers, not a big deal, right? But most plants aren't very old. Whatever they want to show me is quick, just a few images passed over, then it's done. That mistletoe told me everything all at once, and I couldn't handle it. I felt like my brain had short circuited."

Dan moved me so my face was above his. "Short circuited? Did it hurt?"

"No." When he frowned, I shook my head. "It didn't hurt at all. It was more like everything stopped. I shut off."

"Was it a trap set by Moroz?"

"I don't think so. The mistletoe was desperate for help. It didn't mean to come on so strong. I was just the first person it encountered in a long time that was able to understand what it had to say." I caressed his stubbly cheek. He was going on three days' worth of growth, and his whiskers were just transitioning from scratchy to soft. "I like it when you don't shave."

"Maybe I'll grow a beard for you," he said, then he caught my hand. "New rule: you don't touch any more mistletoe, not unless I'm there and you're sitting down. Maybe we can find someone else who talks to plants, and you'll never have to touch it again."

"Are you the plant police now?" I teased.

"No. I'm the officer in charge of protecting one Eliza Lyons." He tucked a length of hair behind my ear. "I can't let anything happen to you. I looked for you my entire life, and now we're finally together."

"Together forever," I added, and he smiled. "I'm not letting anything happen to you, either."

"Look at that. I'm the safest guy in Queens." Dan tucked my face against his neck, and I breathed in his warm, musky scent.

"As scared as I was at the greenhouse, I knew it would be okay," I said. "Even as my brain what shutting down, I knew you would take care of me. I knew you wouldn't let anything hurt me."

"That's right, I won't," he said, then he sighed. "But we do have to talk to the mistletoe again, don't we?"

"It'll be okay," I said with more confidence than I felt. "You'll hold my hand, right?"

Dan tightened his arms around me. "Always, baby."

Chapter Fifteen
All the Pomegranates

My wife and I—man, I love saying that—spent the next hour cleaning up the mess we'd made in the apartment. I took care of putting away the food we hadn't eaten, recycling empty containers, and washing the dishes. While I handled kitchen duty, Eli found a linen closet and put new sheets on the bed, then she dumped the used ones in the washer. Once all that was done, we jumped in the shower. All in all, we made it upstairs just before three in the afternoon.

"I was beginning to wonder if you two were ever coming up for air," Andreas said, when we found him in the sunroom. Eli blushed like crazy, and while that was adorable, I didn't need Andreas teasing her.

"Thanks for letting us hide out downstairs," I said. "We owe you, mostly for all the food we ate."

"Don't worry about it," Andreas said. "Remember how often I had dinner at your place when we were younger? If anything, I owed you. Coffee?"

"Please," Eli said, then she looked around the room. "Where's the mistletoe?"

"I set our new friend up in the dining room," Andreas said, as he brought over two mugs of coffee from the adjoining kitchen. "The sunroom has better light, but the dining room has stronger wards. This way."

We followed Andreas into the dining room. It was a large space with a big bay window in the front, and the window sill was where Andreas had put the fig tree. The mistletoe that had made Eli pass out was sitting on top of the soil, wrapped around the fig's skinny trunk like a leafy scarf.

"Is the asshole attached properly?" I asked.

Eli gave me an exasperated look. "Dan, plants don't have assholes."

"But this one is an asshole," I pointed out.

Andreas laughed into his coffee mug while Eli shrugged. "As far as I know, it should develop a root system that penetrates into the tree bark, but that will take a while," she replied. "Who knows if it can even do that anymore, after being fed blood for so long."

"Do you know whose blood it was?" Andreas asked.

"Not a clue," I replied. "We didn't see any bodies, and no one was there but us and Moroz."

"Interesting," Andreas said. "What would be the purpose of feeding a plant blood?"

"To keep it compliant," Eli said. "I think at least some of the blood was from Moroz. Not all of it, but he wanted to keep the plant under his influence. Blood magic is an easy yet awful way to do that."

"There really wasn't that much blood in the bowl," I said, recalling the shallow pan the mistletoe had been floating in. "If Moroz bleeds himself regularly, a pint or so at a time, it could have been all from him."

Eli nodded, then she stroked the mistletoe's leaves. I braced myself to catch her or throw that stupid plant into the garbage and away from her, but she didn't even stumble. Instead, she glanced at Andreas, and asked, "Would your father have any insight into this?"

"My father?" Andreas demanded, more taken aback than I'd ever seen him. "What makes you think you know anything about my father?"

"He's Hades, right?" Eli pressed. "I mean, your mother is obviously Persephone."

"Obviously?" I repeated. Mama Anastasia was great and all, but she didn't remind me of the goddess of spring.

"Didn't you see all the pomegranates downstairs, and the cornucopia?" Eli asked me, then she turned back to Andreas. "And you gave us those sweatshirts that are basically cloaks of invisibility, and you told us they came from your dad. In the stories, Hades had a cloak of invisibility."

"It's a helm of invisibility, actually." Andreas narrowed his eyes at Eli, then he said to me, "When you said she was brilliant, you didn't say how brilliant."

"Eli is the best investigator you'll ever meet," I said, then I paused. "Is Mama Anastasia really a goddess?"

"I'm not supposed to tell people," Andreas said.

"You didn't," Eli pointed out. "So why isn't she down with your father now, since it's winter and all?"

"They don't keep that up so much any longer," Andreas said. "Besides, the diner's very busy this time of year. I couldn't run it all by myself."

"Does your father ever help?" Eli asked.

Andreas laughed. "He's really only interested in eating food, not preparing it. And before you ask, very few Olympians come by to visit. We always go to them."

Eli's eyes lit up. "You know I'm going to ask you about them."

My phone buzzed, which was great. I needed a distraction from the fact that my childhood best friend was the son of actual gods. I glanced at the screen, and saw a text from Alicia.

Alicia: Danny, where have you been? Everyone's asking about you and Eliza.

Dan: We're good. Had a side trip.

Alicia: Well you two missed a great lunch. Nonna really went all out. And guess what? Remember Mr. Moroz, the Christmas tree guy?

Dan: Yeah
Alicia: He came to visit!

"Hey," I barked. Eli and Andreas stopped their conversation and faced me. "Moroz had lunch with my family." I turned the phone toward them, so they could read the texts.

"Is he still there?" Eli asked.

"Is Alicia all right?" Andreas demanded.

"Let me ask," I said, then I fired off another message.

Dan: Is Moroz still there?
Alicia: No. He left around two.
Alicia: Danny, he offered me a job.
Dan: Doing what?
Alicia: Helping him around the tree farm.

"Moroz offered Alicia a job." I lowered the phone, staring at the last text from my sister. "Never, not once in my entire life, has Moroz gone to Nonna's house."

"He must have been looking for us," Eli said, then she faced Andreas. "You were right about us staying here. Thank you."

Andreas stalked out of the dining room and grabbed his coat from the hall tree. "You can thank me by taking me to your place, and ensuring Moroz never sets foot there again."

I drained my coffee mug and set it on the table. "Let's do it."

Chapter Sixteen
Figs for Christmas

After receiving the texts from Alicia, the four of us—me, Dan, Andreas, and our new friend Mr. Mistletoe—sped across Queens toward Nonna's house. While Dan broke every speed-related traffic law in the state, I told Andreas the rest of the information we'd learned about Moroz, including the hold he had been exerting on Dan's family for the past few decades.

"So basically, it's a geas," I said; not having to explain magical concepts to Andreas was turning out to be quite helpful. "None of Dan's sisters can have kids until all the boys have them first." I watched Andreas fidget in the back seat; he was awfully concerned about Alicia, who Dan claimed he'd drifted away from several years ago. "Maybe they can't have relationships, either. Didn't you used to date Alicia?"

"Yeah," he replied. "We started seeing each other in when we were hardly teenagers. She was a year behind me in school."

"What happened with you two? Did you just grow apart?"

"Nothing happened," Andreas replied. "Absolutely nothing. Things would come up. My family, her family... We tried. I tried. It just never worked out."

"But you love her," I said.

"Yes. I love her." Andreas looked out the window. "But she doesn't love me."

"I'm not so sure that's the case," I said. "Whatever mojo Moroz is laying down, I think it's keeping all of Dan's sisters from having relationships. Moroz has got mad issues stemming from when he killed his daughter, and he's taking them out on Patty's kids"

"Eli's right, man," Dan said. "I remember Alicia going on about you all the way back to middle school. She would probably marry you today, if you asked nicely."

Andreas smiled as he watched the scenery speed past. "I would ask very nicely."

"There's something else I thought of," I continued. "Moroz is looking for a replacement for his daughter, the one that he supposedly accidentally froze to death."

"I don't buy that it was an accident," Dan said.

"Neither do I," I said. "What if he's set his sights on Alicia, and that was what the job offer about her working on the tree farm was really about?"

Andreas let out a string of curses that would have impressed Tessa. "I will destroy him before that happens."

"What if Alicia wants to go work for him?" I asked.

"Why would she want to do that?" Andreas demanded.

"People make weird choices all the time," I said. "Look at Dan. He had a promising career as a police officer, then he shacked up with a seer. His life has been pure chaos ever since."

"Actually," Dan began, "I was having a godawful day at work, then the most beautiful woman I've ever seen walked into the station. I harassed her for two years, then she finally let me kiss her. And here we are today, happily handfasted."

I gave him some side eye. "You were quite the annoying stalker."

"I think you mean effective," Dan said.

"If it's her choice to go with Moroz, I won't stand in her way," Andreas said quietly; our banter definitely wasn't lightening his mood. "But if Alicia refuses him, and he tries to take her against her will, I will move the heavens and the earth itself to keep her safe." He looked up at me, and added, "And no, I won't abduct her and hide her in the underworld. Only my father could pull that off."

I nodded; I hadn't really thought Andreas would resort to kidnapping Alicia if necessary, but it was best to know everyone's intentions up front. "Keeping Alicia safe is now our primary mission."

"Sure is," Dan said, then he pulled into Nonna's driveway.

"How are we going to get the mistletoe inside?" I asked. "It's too cold to leave it in the truck, but we can't exactly wander in with a handful of mistletoe. That would generate all sorts of questions."

"Andreas, grab the whole planter," Dan said. "We'll act like you brought it as a gift for Ma."

"Does Patty like fig trees?" I asked.

"No idea, but Ma likes mistletoe, and she adores Andreas," Dan said. "It'll work, trust me."

We got out of Dan's truck, and unlike our last visit, we bypassed Nonna's kitchen entrance and went in through the front door. We found Dan's parents watching television in the living room while a few of their grandkids played on the floor.

"There's my missing son and his beautiful wife," Patty began, then Andreas stepped out from behind us. "Andreas! You haven't been by in years! Frank, it's Andreas!"

"Good to see you, Andreas," Frank Senior said in his musical voice.

"Forgive me for being a stranger," Andreas said, then he held the fig tree toward Patty. "Peace offering?"

"Oh, I've never seen mistletoe on a fig before," Patty said, as she accepted the tree. "It's quite elegant. Thank you."

"You're very welcome, Mrs. Lyons," Andreas said, then he glanced toward the stairs. "Is Alicia home?"

"I'm not sure," Patty said. "She might have gone out with her sisters. Eliza, would you mind running upstairs to check?"

I blinked. "Me?"

"While I'm sure Andreas remembers exactly where Alicia's room is, no boys are allowed on the second floor unless they're related. We don't need a repeat of what happened after Dan and Andreas's senior prom," Patty added, as Dan laughed and Andreas cleared his throat and looked away. "Second door on the left."

I glanced at Dan. He shrugged, while Andreas refused to make eye contact with me. "Um, okay. I'll be right back."

I went up to the second floor, and did my best to ignore Nonna's first husband's mutterings when I passed him on the landing. If Enzo figured out I could hear him, I'd have a whole new set of problems to deal with, and Nonna seemed to have him under control. I found Alicia's door, and knocked.

"Yeah?"

"It's Eli. Can I come in?"

"Sure."

I pushed the door open, and found Alicia sitting on her bed. Her bedroom was nice, although the pink carpet, matching ruffled bedspread, and frilly white curtains made it seem a little juvenile. Then again, Alicia had lived in this room her entire life. Redecorating probably wasn't her top priority.

"Hey," I said. "Sorry Dan and I have been a bit scarce lately. We were hanging out with an old friend of his."

"It's okay," she said, then she slid over and patted the bed. I sat next to her, and we watched the winter landscape through her window. "We can't expect you guys to be here all the time. You and Danny have an entire life together, unlike the rest of us."

"What does that mean?"

"I only have what's in this house," she replied. "No matter what I do, or how much I try to get out, I'm stuck here. My life begins and ends here."

"Have you considered climbing out the window?" I asked. Alicia smiled, but it didn't reach her eyes. I glanced at the window, and saw that it was nailed shut. Interesting. "Look, I get it. When I was born, it seemed like my entire community had pinned all their hopes and dreams on me. It was stifling, and I while I tried to do everything that was expected of me, I just couldn't do it. It was too much."

"What did you do?" she asked, her eyes wide as saucers. "Did you tell your family it was too much pressure?"

"They got the hint when I walked away," I said. "I didn't leave my family—I really only have my dad, and he's great—but I did walk away from the obligations. I used to be Eli Moore, savior of the world. Now

I'm just regular old Eli, and I have my life with Dan. My life is smaller now, but it's enough." I thought about how Dan and I would slow dance in the kitchen every night after we loaded the dishwasher, and how he had programmed the coffeemaker so we'd wake up to a fresh pot every morning, and smiled. "It's more than enough. It's perfect."

"My life has always been small," Alicia said, a hint of anger in her voice. "I've always been the one waiting. Waiting for Theresa and Dolores to get married and move out, waiting for them to get jobs so then I could do... something."

"Why do you have to wait for them?"

"I'm not really sure," she admitted. "But it's always been that way, the younger ones waits for the older ones to do something first, then we can all do it. Well, all of us except Danny," she added. "He's never let anyone tell him what he could do, or when. He just did it, and we all watched him flourish."

I thought about how Dan was the only one of Patty and Frank's children to move away, and seemingly escape whatever hold Moroz had on the family. Nonna seemed to think Dan had inherited the majority of her Tofana blood, along with aspects from Boreas. Those factors made him somewhat immune to Moroz's influence.

"You can flourish, too," I said. "I'll help you, and so will Dan."

"I wouldn't even know what to do," Alicia said. "I've never had much of a plan for the future. That's why I got so excited when Mr. Moroz offered me a job. I could move out, and have my own life for once."

"Do you want to work for him?"

"Honestly, not really. All I know about Christmas trees is how to decorate them, and I don't know anything about tree farms!"

We laughed together. "I wouldn't want to work there, either. So, what do you want to do? Anything at all, the crazier the better."

"There is one thing... but I don't know if I should tell you," she began. "You're so independent. You'll think I'm old-fashioned or something."

"I won't." I set my hand on her forearm. "Promise."

"Well," Alicia began, leaning toward me as if she was sharing her darkest secret, "I used to have this boyfriend. We got along really well, but then he got busy with his family's business, and I stayed home to help Ma and my sisters, and..." She sighed. "I wasn't enough for him, but I want to be. I want to start talking to him again, and find out if we can make it work."

"Is this busy guy Dan's friend, Andreas?"

"Yeah! Have you met him?"

"I have, and he's downstairs right now."

"What?" Alicia demanded as she shot to her feet. "Why is he here? When did he get here? Is he alone?"

"He came with me and Dan." I stood, and held out my hand. "Come on. He wants to see you."

Alicia worried her lower lip. "You think so?"

"I'm positive. He couldn't stop talking about you on the drive over."

"Well, all right." Tentatively, Alicia took my hand. "Wait, let me change."

"You look great," I said, and she did. Alicia had on a cream colored sweater and jeans, and her dark hair was held back in a clip. "Maybe take down your hair."

Alicia whipped off the hairclip and let her hair fall around her shoulders in loose waves. "Okay. Let's go before I lose my nerve."

"Whatever you say." We stepped into the hallway, and found Enzo pacing the length of it.

"He wants his children," Enzo wailed. "Not my children, but his. His! As if my time with Esme meant nothing."

We walked right past Enzo, which was easy for Alicia. I, on the other hand, felt like my heart was being torn out of my chest. Seeking to give Enzo something good dwell on, I asked Alicia, "Does Nonna ever mention her first husband?"

"You mean Enzo? She talks about him all the time." Alicia led me to the far end of the hall, and showed me a painting of village. Dozens of terra cotta roofs were clustered together on a hillside beneath a clear blue sky. "They were together back in the old country. This is the village where they got married."

"The most beautiful day in history was the day Esme pledged herself to me," Enzo wailed.

"He died before Nonna came to America, but she still tells stories about the adventures they had," Alicia continued. "Get a couple glasses of wine in her, and she'll tell you everything about Enzo."

"That's sweet, that she still thinks about him." Beside us, Enzo placed his ethereal hand on the painting. "True love is strong."

"Love? Bah." Enzo turned to me, his eyes bloodshot. "I wasn't even cold before she found her way to him, and now his children have cursed this family. Cursed! I only wanted happiness."

"Let's go see what's going on downstairs," I said, then I steered Alicia away from the lovesick ghost and toward the stairs. "Andreas brought your mother a fig tree."

"Really?" Alicia asked, as we descended the stairs. "That's a weird…"

Her voice trailed off, so I followed her gaze. Standing in the entrance to the dining room were Dan and his mother. Between them, laughing at something Dan had said, was Andreas.

When Andreas saw Alicia, he went still. "Hi."

I elbowed Alicia. She continued down the stairs, and approached Andreas. "Hi."

"Alicia, Andreas was just saying he would share his recipe for av-golemono soup with us," Patty said, as she sprang into action. "Why don't you help him make some? Right now?"

"But you're the one who wants the recipe," Alicia began, but Match-maker Mom wasn't having it.

"You can tell me how to make it afterward." Patty grabbed Alicia's arm and practically threw her at Andreas. "Go on, now. I'm sure we have all the ingredients in the pantry."

"Would you like to cook with me?" Andreas asked, as he gazed down at Alicia as if she was his world.

"I'd love to," Alicia said, then she took his hand and they entered the kitchen.

"Nice job," I said to Patty, once the kitchen door had closed. "Did you have a hand in your boys finding spouses, too?"

"A mother never tells," Patty said. "I'm going to check on the kids. Don't you dare interfere in there," she warned Dan, with a glare toward the kitchen.

"I won't," he said, as he held up his hands. "Promise." Satisfied, Patty returned to the living room. Once she was out of sight, Dan pulled me into his arms.

"Think Alicia and Andreas will make it work this time?" I asked.

"I hope so. They're good together." Dan rested his chin on the top of my head. "According to Ma, Moroz was only here for about fifteen minutes. He didn't bring anything inside with him, so we don't have to worry about any spelled objects in the house."

"That's good." I remembered my exchange upstairs, and asked, "Is Nonna here? I think we should talk to her."

"She should be in the downstairs kitchen. Think she knows something about why Moroz came by?"

"I think she knows an awful lot, and it's time she shared it with us."

Chapter Seventeen
All the Same Family

While Andreas and Alicia pretended to make soup together, Dan and I went down to Nonna's kitchen. As usual, she was at her stove cooking up a storm. I hoped one of those pots had a protection spell bubbling away in it.

"Buona sera, Nonna," Dan called.

"Too early," Nonna replied. "Say buon giorno, at least until it get dark." Nonna turned around, and frowned at us. "You know Moroz come by?"

"We heard," Dan said. "Everything okay?"

Nonna shook her head. "Nothing okay when he around, but now he gone." We sat at the counter, and she presented us with a plate of her homemade almond cookies. "How you two? You eat yet?"

"We ate at Andreas's place," Dan replied, with such a straight face I was certain he was messing with me.

"Then cookies for snack," Nonna said. "I make fresh coffee."

"Andreas came here with us, to talk to Alicia," Dan said. Nonna smiled, and murmured that those two were good together.

"When I went upstairs to get Alicia, Enzo talked to me," I said; I needed to steer the conversation away from Andreas and absolutely everything that happened at his house. Otherwise, my face would end up as red as a tomato. "He implied that Moroz had cursed this family, all because of something that happened with someone else's children."

Nonna sighed. "Enzo still mad he dead. He try to get me in trouble." She bustled around her kitchen for a moment, and we didn't rush her to answer. One thing Dan and I had both cultivated during our careers as investigators was patience.

"I no kill Enzo," she said at length.

"I never thought you did," I replied.

"He had fever. I tried to save him." Nonna turned away, and busied herself organizing the serving spoons in a crock on the counter. "He think because I seer, I could have try harder."

"Could you have?" Dan asked.

"I try everything," Nonna said softly. "Magic, medicine, nothing work. You know, piccolina," Nonna added, turning to face me. "Some-time, when nothing work, it time to move on."

"It's true." I remembered my gran's last few days. Even though she was the Matriarch and the most powerful seer in the world, she could do nothing to stop her own spirit from leaving her body. "The last thing my grandmother said to me before she died was that death wasn't something to fear. It was just another door to step through."

Dan grunted. "Then what's Enzo scared of?"

"Enzo scared to be alone," Nonna replied. "What he say to you, piccolina. Enzo no mean my children. He mean Boreas's children."

"You mean Frank Senior?" I asked.

"No. Boreas had children before I knew him. One of his sons, Davos, he meet a girl called Natasha. He love her, but Natasha's father no approve. He freeze both of them till they die, though he only mean to freeze Davos. And that is why Moroz hates our family. He blame Boreas for the loss of his daughter."

"Wait a second," Dan said. "This Natasha is the daughter Moroz killed?"

"Si," Nonna replied. "After Natasha meet Davos she spend all her time with him. Moroz jealous, so he kill boy." She shook her head. "Boreas so sad after Davos die. I try to help, but what could I do? A parent should never have to bury their child."

Dan reached across the counter and set his hand on Nonna's. She turned her palm up and squeezed his hand in return. "Where were you and Boreas when this happened?" Dan asked. "Back in Europe?"

"No, we here," Nonna replied. "We already live in this house."

Dan and I glanced at each other. "So, all of this happened not that long ago?" Dan asked.

Nonna shrugged. "Feel like yesterday. After Davos die, Boreas leave for a while. He need time to grieve, and I give it to him. Frank born half a year later."

"Then Moroz found some of Boreas's descendants, set up a tree farm slash mistletoe production center, and bided his time until Patty and Frank Senior needed a Christmas tree," I deduced. "Moroz is nothing but a lame villain with an overly complicated plan for revenge."

"Why didn't you ever try to get rid of him?" Dan asked Nonna. "Slip him some Acqua Tofana, something like that?"

"Danny, if I try that, then he know I seer," Nonna replied. "Moroz suspect, but he no certain. Even so, he drive all the witches away, so I have no one to turn to for help. All I can do is stay here, and keep the house and everyone in it safe."

"Then the farm isn't warded against seers," I said, as Nonna's words solved yet another mystery. "The first time Dan and I went up to Maple Acres, this crazy cold wind tried blowing me away. Moroz was surprised I made it inside his shop—but he wasn't surprised because a seer beat his wards. He was shocked that a witch made it through."

Nonna regarded me, her head tilted to the side and her brows pinched. "But, you Helena's granddaughter," she said. "Mistress of Seers."

"That's true, but my mother is a witch," I said.

Nonna nodded. "Then you have advantage."

"Witches must be his Achilles heel," Dan said. "Maybe we should loop in Tess."

"We should give her a heads up, but we need to do something now," I said. "The fact that Moroz came to the house means he's stepping up his plan." I turned to Nonna, and said, "We think he wants to replace Natasha with Alicia."

"Never," Nonna said, with an edge to her voice I hadn't heard before. "The things he do to Natasha were evil. I kill him with my bare hands before I let him touch Alicia."

"We can hide her," Dan said. "Although, that's going to be hard until after Christmas. If she's not at all the family events it'll look suspicious, and we don't need extra scrutiny with Moroz already sniffing around."

"That, and if Moroz pops in again and she isn't home, he might start looking for her," I said. "If he has access to some sort of locator spell, and Alicia's alone when he finds her, who knows what will happen."

"Then what do we do?" Dan asked.

What, indeed. As I wracked my brain for ideas, my gaze traveled around the kitchen, and landed on Nonna's spice cabinet. Specifically, the shelf where she kept the Acqua Tofana.

"Nonna, when you poisoned me, I had a vision," I said. "I went out to the greenhouse, and even though it was winter, everything inside was green and growing. I looked through the plants, and saw belladonnas growing with the tomatoes. A man appeared behind me, and said the plants are in the same family. What do you think that means?"

"Hmm." She retreated to her stove, and tended to her bubbling pots while she thought. "This man. What he look like?"

"Strong," I replied. "He was tall, had dark hair, and a beard. Actually, he looked a lot like Dan."

"Boreas," Nonna said; even though her back was to us, I could hear the smile in her voice. "Danny look much like my Boreas."

Dan kissed my temple, and murmured, "Now I am definitely growing that beard."

I smiled at my vain husband. "Why would Boreas hop into my vision, and talk about families?"

Nonna shrugged. "The best way to learn, is to have vision again and ask him yourself."

"You mean have Eli take more of that poison?" Dan asked. "That's a no."

"Dan—"

"Absolutely not," he said over me, as he made a cutting motion with his hand. "Not even twenty-four hours ago, I watched you touch a freaky plant and faint dead away. No way are you doing that again willingly."

"I don't need to take poison in order to have a vision," I said, a bit exasperated at his protective nature. "I can put myself into a trance."

"If Eli do trance, you can follow," Nonna said, then she tapped the mark I'd tattooed onto Dan's wrist. "Now that you open to magic, you can protect her on spiritual plane, too."

"I can?" Dan looked from his wrist, to me.

"It's really not hard to go into a trance and enter the astral plane," I said. "And we're already linked, thanks to the handfasting. You should be able to follow me, easy peasy."

He frowned, at looked to Nonna for clarification. "Listen to your wife," Nonna said. "She go, you follow. I get a nice herbal tea together to help you. No poison," she added, as she waggled a finger at Dan.

We watched Nonna head over to her spice cabinet, then Dan took my hands. "You're sure about this?"

"Sure we'll get answers? No. But I am certain I can induce a trance, and I'm also certain you can follow me." I scooted closer, so our knees touched. "And I know—I'm not just certain but I know, deep in my heart—that you won't let anything happen to me while we're on the astral plane, just like I'll protect you. What do you say? Want to go on a trance with me?"

He blew out a breath. "Trance it is."

Chapter Eighteen
A Greenhouse in Winter

I did not like this.

Eli had gone into trances a few times since we'd met. Sometimes they were planned, sometimes they weren't, but each and every time it killed me to watch her go motionless and nonresponsive. Still, I'd always kept my objections to myself, and stood guard over Eli's body until she was awake and in my arms again. Now she was going to induce another trance, this time to try and speak to Boreas. Today's trance was different for two reasons.

One, this would be the first time she intentionally went under since she destroyed Amir Hassan's soul on the astral plane. He was her cold-blooded, evil ex who'd tried to steal her birthright as the leader of the seer community, and murdered several people in the process.

Eli had come out of that trance in tears, convinced that now she was a murderer. As for me, I thought Hassan had earned his fate, and I tried to reassure Eli that she'd done the right thing. In her mind, she knew she'd been in the right, but her heart still hurt.

And two, when Eli had passed out after touching the mistletoe at Moroz's tree farm, for a split second I thought she'd dropped dead in front of my eyes.

I've got more baggage than the average bear, and a lot of it has to do with my first wife, Charlotte. She'd been a beautiful, sweet, smart ray of sunshine. Char had also been very, very sick. One day, when we thought she was getting better, she stood up from the kitchen table and smiled at me.

Then she went upstairs and died. Right there in our house, she died, and for the longest time, I was convinced my heart had died with her. I went through the motions of life for about three years, and I barely survived. Then I met Eli, my beautiful Eliza, and learned that second chances were a real thing.

There was no way I would let my second chance with Eli end, not for anything in the world.

Nonna set a cup of something hot in front of me. "What's that?" I asked.

"Passionflower," Nonna replied. "It help trance. No worry, I no put poison in it."

"I know, Nonna. When I said that earlier, I was just worried about Eli."

"I understand." Nonna patted my hand. "Love make us act strange, eh?"

"You're right about that." I drew the mug toward me, and smelled the tea. It was a heavy floral scent, with a bit of citrus. I wondered if that was natural, or if Nonna had added a lemon to the pot. "Think we'll see Boreas when we go under?"

"Maybe," she allowed. "If so, you lucky. He very protective of his children, like you protective of yours."

"Nonna, I don't have any kids."

She patted my hand again. "Patience, Danny."

Eli picked that moment to return from the bathroom. Her eyes were bright and shining, and her nose was pink. She'd been crying. After she sat on a stool next to me, I leaned toward her, and whispered, "Talk to me, baby."

"I'm okay," she said, then she flashed me a smile. "I was remembering everything that happened with Amir."

"Wasn't your fault," I began, then she held up her hand.

"I know, but I wanted to get those emotions out now. I don't want to drag old hurts onto the astral plane with us."

I nodded, wondering what exactly would happen to us if we got upset when we were floating spirits, but resisted the urge to ask her too much. We could talk about these old hurts later, when we were alone. "You're sure about this?"

"I am," she said, then she took my hand and squeezed. "Something or someone here wants to talk to me. Might as well find out what they have to say."

I still didn't like the idea of us going under, but I trusted Eli and Nonna. "Do we need a safe word? So we know to retreat?"

"We can't just say 'retreat'?" she asked.

My wife was a smartass, and I loved her even more because of it. "All right, we can do that. How do we start?"

Eli smelled the mug of tea. "What's in here besides passionflower?" she asked Nonna.

"You kids too suspicious," Nonna said. "Just tea!"

"Okay." Eli took a sip from the cup, then she slid it toward me. "Go on. Drink."

I did. The tea had cooled off, but it was all right. A little too herbal for my tastes, but I wasn't drinking it for the flavor. "Now what?"

"Close your eyes." I did, and felt Eli take my hands. "Can you feel your heart beating?"

"Yeah. I can."

"Good. Now find mine."

"How can I hear your heartbeat all the way over here?"

"Just try."

I bit back my next response, and did as asked. My own heartbeat was a drum solo in my chest, thanks to my anxiety over Eli going under again. Add to that the blood rushing through my ears, and I was a symphony of nerves. Just as I was about to announce my complete and utter failure at noticing anything outside my own body, I heard something else.

Something in the background.

It was softer, the rhythm faster than my own heartbeat... then I realized what I was listening to.

Eli's heartbeat.

I found it.

"I've got you, babe," I said. "I can hear you, clear as day."

A gentle squeeze of my hands. "Good. Now follow me."

"How? We're sitting down."

"Not my body. Follow my heartbeat."

"All right," I said, even as I wondered if I could even do that. I trained my ears to Eli's heartbeat, and let the gentle thumps pull me along. It wasn't long before the sound was accompanied by a shimmering silver rope that I saw not with my eyes, but in my mind. I grabbed onto the rope and pulled myself forward, until my astral form bumped into Eli's.

"See?" she said, and she pulled me into her arms. "Just like I told you. We were already linked."

"Look at that." Now that we were in contact, the rope faded away, but a silver glow remained around us. "So, this is the astral plane?"

"It sure is. Look. There we are." Eli pointed toward the counter, and I saw our bodies slumped toward each other. Nonna was standing at her stove, but kept glancing over her shoulder to keep an eye on us.

"It's like we're in an old movie," I said. Everything was in black and white, except for Eli. Her rich brown hair and freckled skin were as vibrant as ever.

"Not sure why I'm the only thing in technicolor. Usually I'm as washed out as everything else," she said, then she shrugged. "But we can worry about that later. Let's go to the greenhouse."

We exited through the kitchen's side door, and just like it had been for Eli's last vision, we discovered that the greenhouse was not shut down for the season. Instead, it was up and running and packed with vegetables. Even stranger, it was still winter in the yard, and snow was piled up against the greenhouse in drifts.

"Weird," I said, as I looked through the glass walls at all the produce waiting to be picked. "It's winter out here, and summer in there."

"Boreas's influence, maybe?" Eli suggested, then a frigid wind came out of nowhere and chilled me to my bones. I pulled Eli into my arms on the pretext of keeping her warm, but I really just loved holding her, though her gaze was fixed over my shoulder. "Dan, it's him."

I turned around, and saw a very tall, very muscular man standing on the path behind us. He did have dark hair and a full beard, and his arms were crossed over his chest.

"Boreas?" I asked, mostly because he was wearing a flannel shirt and jeans, instead of the togas Greek gods are usually depicted in. I guessed it was too cold this time of year for that sort of get up.

Boreas acknowledged me with a curt nod. "Esme sent you?"

"The first time, yes," Eli replied. "This trip was my idea. Moroz is messing with your family, I think for the second time."

Boreas scowled. "That demon has earned my eternal ire. He could not accept that his daughter was grown, and wanted a life of her own with Davos. Now she is beyond his reach, and it galls him that he cannot control her."

"What do you mean by beyond his reach?" I asked. "I thought Moroz froze her to death."

"He did, but I rescued Davos and Natasha's souls before they made the journey to hades," Boreas explained. "I transformed them into winter winds, so they may spend eternity together. They chase each other across the mountains, free from Moroz's vengeance."

"That's great," I said, and Boreas frowned. Like an ass, I'd just implied that it was great his son was dead. Eli's hand tightened on mine, which was good. I needed the support. "However, now Moroz is after my—our—family."

"He has a very old mistletoe specimen," Eli continued. "And with that specimen, he has placed a geas on Dan's sisters. We're pretty sure he wants to take one of them as a replacement for Natasha."

"Moroz's power isn't in the mistletoe," Boreas said. "He has an enchanted shard of ice. Break the shard, break the power."

"Sounds easy enough," I said. "Any idea where this shard is?"

"It's on his person, or close to him," Boreas replied. "He can only tap into its power when he holds the shard against his skin."

"All right," I said. "We've got a new plan. Thank you."

Boreas dipped his chin. "Do not hesitate to call on me, Daniel, for any sort of aid I may offer you. Esme has often said that you alone of your siblings inherited the bulk of our abilities. Now I see that you've claimed the Mistress of Seers as your bride, and I know her heart to be true and her power strong. However, others will sense your power, and with greater power comes greater threats to you and yours."

"Like Moroz harassing my sisters?" I asked.

"Not this family," Boreas said, with a shake of his head. "With the new family you are building with Eliza. Be cautious, my son."

With that, Boreas faded from view. "Looks like a god just told me I better take good care of you," I said, as I draped my arm around Eli's shoulders.

"How did he know I'm Mistress of Seers?" she murmured. "Think Nonna told him?"

"Maybe." I pressed my face against her hair. Eli's hair always smelled amazing, no matter what kind of shampoo she used. "You know I'll always take care of you, right?"

"Of course I do." She sighed, and turned into my arms. "While you're taking care of me, we need to figure out how to divest Moroz of his magic ice cube. How are we going to do that?"

"Hit him with a blast from a blow dryer?" I suggested.

"Hmm. That would melt the ice, at least a little bit."

"I was kidding!"

"But it could work." Eli burrowed deeper into my arms. "Actually, now that I think about it, it probably wouldn't. If he keeps the ice on him, it might be magically resistant to melting."

"Melt proof ice. Who would have thought." I kissed Eli's hair. "When should we go back to our bodies?"

"We already accomplished what we set out to do, so we might as well go now," she replied, her breath warm against my throat. "Unless you want to spy on Alicia and Andreas?"

"A world of no," I said, then I thought of something. "Can we spy on Moroz this way?"

"We can, but it might not be a good idea," she replied. "Some beings can sense when spirits are nearby, including those projecting like we are. It's similar to how I sense spirits. Since we don't understand the full extent of Moroz's abilities, I think it's best we keep our spirits away from him."

"We can't sneak up on him?"

She shook her head. "Not until we know more about him. Otherwise, it's too dangerous."

And if there was anything I wouldn't do, it was put Eli in danger. She managed that well enough on her own. "All right, babe. Let's go inside, and find out what Ma's making for dinner."

Chapter Nineteen
The Incident

Dinner turned out to be a simple meal featuring the fettuccini that I helped make with Dan's mother the day before. No one mentioned the uneven shapes of the noodles, which was nice. Patty served it with a tomato cream sauce, grilled chicken, and a green salad. Dessert was more of Nonna's incredibly delicious almond cookies. I didn't think I could ever get enough of those little treats. All in all, it was a nice family dinner, made all the nicer because I felt like I belonged.

However, most of the family wasn't even at dinner. None of Dan's brothers or their wives were present, which meant no grandkids, either. While they were missed, the most scandalous absence of the evening was Alicia. When Dan and I were talking to Boreas on the astral plane, Andreas and Alicia had left together. They hadn't told anyone where they were going—they were adults, after all—or when they would be back.

"Can't be gone too long," Dan said, as he grabbed another cookie. "It's Christmas Eve tomorrow."

"He wouldn't keep her out all night," Dolores said. "Would he?"

"Of course not," Theresa said. "That's not right."

"And Andreas has manners," Patty added, as she stood and gathered up some plates for the dishwasher. "He'll bring Alicia home soon."

"They didn't even finish the soup they were making," Theresa added, after Patty was in the kitchen. I bit the inside of my cheek, since soup clearly hadn't been on either of their minds. I also wondered if either of Dan's older sisters had ever actually been on a date. They were behaving like characters from a historical romance who'd never been in a room with a boy unchaperoned.

"You craving some soup, T?" Dan asked. "I bet there's a can of chicken noodle around here somewhere."

The look Theresa gave Dan could have stopped a clock. "You know this isn't about soup," she snapped. "I remember what you and Andreas were like when you were younger, Danny. I remember *the incident*."

"Ooo, there was an incident?" I asked. "I wanna hear."

"Ma's forbidden us from mentioning it ever again," Dolores said, then she tossed a glare at Dan. "It was disgraceful."

"Shameful," Theresa added.

I turned to Dan. "Is it bad that now I want to know ever more?"

Dan squeezed my hand, then he pushed back from the table. "That's our cue to leave," he said. "I know better than to start talking about the forbidden incident two days before Christmas. See you all tomorrow."

We said our goodbyes to everyone, then we got in Dan's truck and headed back to the hotel. "Your family is really great," I said.

"They are." Dan glanced at me, then he turned onto the main street. Out of habit, I looked in the side mirror, and saw the car behind us make the same turn. "I assume you want to know everything that happened during the incident in question."

"Yes!"

"It was the night of my and Andreas's senior prom," he began. "Alicia and Andreas were just getting serious, and he invited her to prom—but Ma didn't want Alicia to go. Thought she was too young, all of that."

"They're only a year apart," I pointed out, rather unnecessarily. "They're closer in age than we are."

"I hear ya," Dan said. "As you know, I've always been Alicia's partner in crime. So, I engineered a distraction, Alicia climbed out her window, and she went to the dance with Andreas."

"That was daring. Is that why her bedroom window is nailed shut?"

"Not quite. See, Ma never knew Alicia was gone. She thought her youngest child was upstairs, sleeping in her bed like a good girl. Well, next morning she opens Alicia's door and finds Andreas bare assed in her room!"

"Holy cow," I squealed. "Your mother must have turned purple!"

"Purple, red, all the colors," Dan said. "Anyway, that's the incident, and it's also why boys aren't allowed on the second floor."

"Did you get in trouble?"

"Me? Never." He flashed me a sly smile. "I always have an alibi."

"Golden boy Danny," I teased, then my foresight crackled. I glanced at the side view mirror, and saw a white sedan behind us. I remembered seeing the same car pull out behind us when we turned off of Nonna's street. "You see the car behind us?"

"Yep. It's been back there for a while now. Wanna take a tour of New York? I don't want to lead this person back to our hotel."

"Sure. Or we could stop somewhere well-lit, and try to draw this person out," I said. "I don't have the patience for sneakiness."

"Whatever you say, babe," Dan said, then he cut the wheel and made a u-turn in the middle of the road.

"What the hell?" I demanded, as horns honked and tires screeched around us.

"I wanted to see if he would follow a move like that," Dan replied, then he checked the rearview mirror. "And he did."

"We could pull in here," I said, indicating an empty parking lot.

"Nah. Let's see how long he'll keep up with us."

"Dan," I began, but he shook his head.

"The longer he follows us, the more keyed up he'll be," Dan said. "That means he might make a mistake."

"He might also shoot us," I pointed out.

"If he shoots, I shoot back. I've still got plenty of friends on the force, and if we need them I'll call in every favor I'm owed." Dan stopped at a red light. "You trust me?"

I leaned over the console and set my hand on his cheek, turning his face to mine. "You know I do," I said, then I kissed him. I saw the light change to green in my peripheral vision. "Go. Wind the bastard up."

Dan grinned, then he proceeded through the intersection. "Maybe I'll take him through Midtown."

"Do you think it's weird that we had a sex marathon this morning?" I asked, because being followed by an unknown person was a great time to discuss our love life.

"You want to talk about that now?"

"I've got time. Besides, it's been bugging me."

"Bugging you how? Was it... was it bad? Or painful?"

"No to both," I replied; Dan was a lot bigger than me, and he was always worried that if we got too rough, he might hurt me. He never had, not even accidentally. "It was awesome. You know that."

I saw his jaw relax, and let myself exhale. "Was it too sticky, then?"

Laughter bubbled out of my throat. "That was also great, but the honey is part of the weirdness. I mean, we're pretty affectionate, but this morning was like we were starting our own porn empire."

"It was pretty intense," Dan admitted. "Honestly, I thought it was due to all the adrenaline from sneaking around the farm and stealing Moroz's stash."

"That's probably a big part of it," I said. "But we were in Persephone's house."

"I still can't wrap my mind around that," Dan said, then he cut the wheel for another tight left turn. Behind us, the white sedan did the same. "Are you wondering if Persephone influenced us?"

"Not directly, but she is the goddess of spring," I said. "Green and growing things."

"Maybe bringing the freaky mistletoe into her house set something off."

"Maybe." I assessed our surroundings. Dan had taken us to a part of the city I'd never seen before, and there was a rotary up ahead. In the center of the rotary was a circular park with a statue on a tall pillar. I pointed toward the monument, and asked, "What's that?"

"Columbus Circle. And I'm sick of being chased." Dan hooked the wheel, and drove up the pedestrian walkway toward the central statue.

"I don't think you're supposed to drive here," I shrieked.

"No, this is definitely frowned upon." Dan slammed on the brakes, causing our follower to do the same. It was a wonder we weren't rear ended. The truck was still rolling when Dan leapt out of it and approached the sedan with his gun drawn.

"Out of the car," Dan yelled. "Now!"

"Danny, everyone knows you're not a police officer any longer," Moroz said as he exited the sedan.

"Cop or not, I've still got the gun." Dan used his gun to wave Moroz away from the car. Once he was a few steps away, Dan slammed the sedan's door shut. "Why are you following us?"

"Where is my mistletoe?" Moroz demanded.

"We don't have it," I said, as I came around the truck to stand beside Dan. "Also, plant torture is a new and disgusting talent I've never experienced before."

"What are you?" Moroz demanded. "No witch should have been able to breach my farm, and yet you did. Twice now, if I'm not mistaken."

I shrugged. "What can I say. I've never been one to follow rules."

Moroz shook his head. "No, it's not that," he said, as he took a step toward me. I heard the safety click off on Dan's gun. "You remind me of my Natasha."

"And the creepy gets kicked up a notch," I said.

"Natasha's mother was the strongest seer in Volgoda," Moroz continued, as he took another step toward me. "She, too, could talk to plants, and make them do her bidding. You, Eliza, made my mistletoe scream."

"Take another step toward Eli and I will blow your fucking head off," Dan yelled. "Why have you been messing with my family?"

Moroz's icy gaze turned to Dan. "I require a new daughter. Once, I thought I located the ideal candidate, but now I've found another," he said, then ice erupted from the perimeter of the circle. Too late, I realized the area was ringed in fountains, which had been shut down for the winter, but the plumbing must have remained connected. Before I could scream or speak or even breathe, I was covered in ice.

Chapter Twenty
Thawing Out

One second, I was screaming at Moroz to get away from Eli.

Then the fountains exploded, and I was soaked in cold water that instantly turned to ice. In less than a minute, I was frozen solid. Then I saw lights.

Red lights.

By some supreme stroke of luck, an ambulance had been passing by Columbus Circle just as Moroz set off the fountains and created the ice show of all ice shows. The paramedics got to me and Eli within a few minutes, and they hauled us off the ice and wrapped us in thermal blankets. If they hadn't been nearby, we might have frozen to death.

As we thawed out, more responders arrived on scene. A cop brought us some hot chocolates, then another officer recognized me and called my brother, who happened to be the supervising officer on duty that night. By the time Carmelo arrived, I almost had the feeling back in my toes. He stood over us, scowling, as Eli drank her hot chocolate and politely answered the paramedic's questions. My brother, he had questions of his own.

"What the hell happened?" Carmelo demanded, as soon as we'd walked out of earshot of the rest. "The firefighters say the fountain's pipes exploded and caused black ice, and your truck lost control and skidded up here."

"That sounds plausible," I said.

"It is, if you ignore the fact that you and Eliza were found by paramedics outside of your truck," Carmelo said. "And they both saw the fountains explode, and you two were already in the circle."

"Did they say that?" I surveyed the scene. At least a dozen first responder vehicles had arrived, and the light show was impressive. "Hm."

"No bullshit, baby brother," Carmelo said. "What happened?"

I wiped my hand down my face. "If I tell you, you'll think I'm nuts."

"Try me." When I stayed quiet, he continued, "Listen, the report is going to say that the water leak from bad plumbing created a shit ton of ice and made you lose control of your vehicle. Wouldn't be the first time old city pipes burst at a public fountain during winter."

"Thanks, man."

"But I want to know what really happened." Carmelo crossed his arms over his chest. "Your gun is in my car. The paramedics found it in your hand after they got you and Eli in the ambulance. The safety was off," he added.

I blew out a breath, and prepared to tell Carmelo a story he might not believe. "Moroz, the Christmas tree guy? He's after Alicia."

Carmelo blinked. "The old guy Ma gets decorations from? The one that came by for lunch today?"

"Yeah. He's got a delusion that Alicia can replace his deceased daughter. Also, he's got some weird power over the cold."

"What, like Mr. Freeze?"

"Something like that. When Eli and I left Nonna's after dinner, Moroz followed us. When we realized what was happening, I led him here. He got out of his car, we did the same, and he told us he found someone to be his new daughter." I gestured toward the frozen circle. "Then the fricken' pipes blew."

"Shit." Carmelo ran his hand over his hair. "You're serious."

"As a heart attack," I said, then I realized something. "You believe me about Moroz?"

"Of course I do," he said. "You wouldn't make up someone being after Alicia, and you sure as hell wouldn't turn yourself into an ice cube just to fuck around."

"True. So, what's our move?"

Carmelo grunted, then he turned around to assess the scene. "Where's Moroz's car?"

"He must have fled. It was a white sedan, late model."

"You get a plate?"

"No, but I bet Eli did," I said, as we started walking back to the ambulance. "She's been a private investigator for years. No detail gets past her."

"Figures. Danny had to get himself the second most brilliant and beautiful woman in the world for a wife."

I stopped walking. "Second?"

"Graciela will always be number one for me," he said, and I didn't argue. Carmelo and Graciela had been together for decades, and were devoted to each other. Always had been.

We reached the ambulance, where my own beautiful and brilliant wife sipped her watery hot chocolate as she sat on the bumper. The color was back in her cheeks, which was a good sign. "Babe, Carmelo's got a few questions."

She set her cup aside and faced him. "What do you need to know?"

"A lot," Carmelo said, as he gave me some side eye, "But first, did you get a look at the sedan's plate?"

"Sure did," she replied, then she gave Carmelo not only Moroz's license plate number, but the year, make, and model of the vehicle.

"We didn't see that car at the tree farm," she continued. "It was a New York plate, but I suspect it might not be registered in his name."

"Good work, kid," Carmelo said, as he scribbled the information down in his notepad. "You ever think about moving to the city and becoming a cop? Seems like a waste of your skills to have you out in cow country."

"Me? A cop?" Eli laughed. "That's funny."

"Well, if you ever change your mind, let me know." Carmelo faced me. "Give me your keys."

"Are you impounding my truck?" I asked.

"No. I'm going to take your truck, and you're going to take my car." When I hesitated, Carmelo said, "Listen, this guy knows your ride, and he knows Nonna's place, but I'm betting he doesn't know my car, or where you're staying. Let's get a leg up on the asshole and throw him off the trail."

"All right," I said, as I handed my keys over. "What do you want us to do?"

"Tonight? Nothing. I'll put a squad car near Nonna's to keep an eye on everything. Tomorrow, we watch Alicia like a hawk."

"She's not at home," I said. "Her and Andreas took off together earlier this afternoon."

"Andreas, huh? They're rekindling old flames for the holidays?"

"Seems so," I replied. "They were pretty happy to see each other."

"Then Theresa mentioned the incident," Eli chimed in.

"We don't talk about that," Carmelo said, and Eli grinned. She loved family drama. "But seriously, I'll swing by the diner and see if those two are there. Don't worry, baby brother. We'll keep everyone safe, and we'll nail this dickhead, too."

CHAPTER TWENTY-ONE
BREAKFAST BUFFET

The next morning, I woke up shivering.

That was just weird, since I was in bed with Dan. Even if we hadn't been lying beneath two blankets and the super fluffy hotel comforter, he gave off enough body heat to warm an entire house. Me shivering wasn't just unusual, it bordered on scientifically impossible.

But we weren't dealing with science, and magic cared little for the laws of physics. When Moroz had caused the pipes to burst at Columbus Circle and shower us in ice cold water, a fair amount had frozen right onto our bodies. I'd been standing on Dan's left, which meant I got the brunt of the ice storm. The paramedics had gotten to us pretty fast, and the ice melted away once we were under the thermal blankets. That left us soaking wet and shivering on a cold winter night.

Even though we'd both taken hot showers once we got back to our hotel room, I still felt like I had frost in my veins.

I got out of bed, threw on Dan's sweatshirt, some wool socks, and a pair of fleece leggings, and started the hotel room's coffee maker. Once that was going, I put my hair up in a ponytail—I used a purple scrunchie, since in my world purple was the most festive color and this was the holiday season—and checked the thermostat. It read seventy-two degrees, so I left it alone, even though I really wanted to crank it up to eighty. As I willed the coffee to brew faster, Dan woke up.

"Hey," he said, when he saw me. "You're already dressed?"

"I was cold."

He pulled the comforter aside. "Then come back here."

I did, and soon enough, I was wrapped in his arms. "Better?" he asked.

"Better," I replied, leaving off how while I was warmer now that I was back in bed, I still wouldn't call myself warm. "I think Moroz's ice storm had an after effect, if you know what I mean."

"I get it, baby." A soft kiss against my hair. "What we need is a nice hot breakfast to warm us from the inside out."

"That's a great idea. Diner pancakes?"

"Yeah, but not Andreas's diner. He might think we're spying on him and Alicia, especially since Carmelo went by there last night."

I laughed against his chest. "Well, we don't want to scare them away from each other, though I don't think that would happen. When Alicia found out Andreas was there at Nonna's yesterday, she got so excited she almost jumped out of her skin."

"You know how us Lyons are," he said. "We find our one true love, and stalk them until they love us back."

"You were a very slow stalker," I said; Dan had kept things professional between us for years.

"You never gave me any hint that you were interested," he countered. "For years I was begging for the slightest crumbs of your attention, then I find out you and Tessa were calling me Officer Muscleman behind my back."

"That was all Tess," I said. "Once, back when we first met, when you came by my office, you took off your jacket and rolled up your sleeves. She talked about your muscular forearms for days afterward."

"Forearms. So that's what women like." Dan grabbed his phone.

"What are you doing?"

"Ordering more short sleeved shirts. I gotta keep the ladies happy."

I giggled against his chest, but didn't try to stop him. He did look pretty good in a tee shirt. "I take it a yummy diner breakfast is off the table, Officer Muscleman?"

"Just for today. Want to order room service?"

"Sure. I've got the app saved." I rolled out of his arms, grabbed my phone, and brought up the room service menu. "Small change. There's no room service today. Instead, there's an extra special festive Christmas Eve buffet happening downstairs."

"All right," Dan said. "Let me grab a shower, then we can go down to eat."

"I'm already dressed. I can go get us breakfast, and bring it back up while you shower."

Dan stroked my hair back from my forehead. "You take pretty good care of me, Mrs. Lyons."

"I learned from the best, Mr. Lyons." I reluctantly left the bed again, and started putting on my shoes. "After we eat, I guess we'll have to decide what to do about Moroz's latest nonsense."

"After my shower, I'll call Carmelo, see if he made any headway," Dan said. "One of the squad cars might have seen something."

"Hopefully someone arrested him, and we can all move on." Shoes now on, I headed toward the door. "Any breakfast requests?"

"Anything with bacon is fine with me."

"Bacon it is. Back in a flash." I left our room, and walked down the corridor toward the elevator. I was still smiling when I got to the lobby, and smelled the wonderful breakfast aromas of baked goods and coffee wafting out of the hotel restaurant. I couldn't think of a better way to celebrate Christmas Eve that sharing pancakes in bed with Dan.

Then I shivered.

No, I shuddered, with a chill that I felt all the way down to my bones. Figuring I was standing too close to an air vent, I ignored it and continued on toward the restaurant. Even when I entered the room, which was as warm and cheery as a place could be the day before Christmas, I couldn't shake the chill. Assuming it was a case of leftover trauma from being frozen the night before, I shook it off and headed toward the hostess stand. After I gave her my name so the room could be charged for our food, the hostess gave me two to-go containers and told me to take as much as I wanted, and that I was welcome to come back for more.

"If I eat more than can fit in one of these containers, I might pop," I said.

"You're supposed to overeat during the holidays," the hostess said. "It's practically a rule."

"I like the way you think," I said, then I approached the buffet. As I was about to start filling the containers, ice cold fingers clamped down on my shoulder and a voice growled close to my ear.

"You're coming with me, my snowy girl."

Chapter Twenty-Two
Foresight

Even though Eli wasn't in the shower with me, I still made sure the water was almost unbearably hot. Either she was rubbing off on me, or Moroz really had frozen us on a cellular level. I was hoping for the former.

The kicker was that ever though we'd only been separated for five minutes, I already missed Eli. As much as I joked about how it took her years to warm up to me, I'd fallen hard and fast for Eli. I would have asked her out the day we met, if we hadn't met at the police station. I'd been assigned to take statement about a case she'd been involved in. I will never forget when I went out to the waiting area, and saw an absolutely gorgeous woman sitting patiently near the windows. We went into one of the interrogation rooms so I could take her statement, then she proceeded to make fun of my name, and explain how she caught a serial killer that had left a trail of bodies across three states. By the time Eli left the station that day, I was already head over heels in love with her.

And now we were married, and my family loved her, and I was totally allowed to miss her when I showered by myself. Never in a million years had I thought I'd meet someone like Eli, who complimented me in every way. I liked to think that I complimented her, too, and we brought out the best in each other. Although, to me, she was already perfect.

Five minutes later, I got out of the shower, dried off, and got on the phone with Carmelo. He had nothing to report, either from the squad car sent to watch Nonna's, or from his stop at the diner last night. In fact, he hadn't seen Alicia or Andreas at the diner, which probably meant those two had stayed in. That meant Alicia was safe, and we could all take a moment to breathe. Since everything seemed calm for the moment, I sent Alicia a text.

Dan: Merry Christmas Eve, little sis.
Dan: You up?

I waited a full five minutes for her to reply. Nothing. Wondering if she was also getting ready for the day, I texted Andreas.

Dan: Morning! You working today?
Dan: Eli can't stop talking about your pancakes. We're having breakfast at the hotel this morning, and she is not pleased about that.

Crickets. Hoping those two had better things to do than send me messages, I straightened up the bed. As I put the pillows back where they belonged, I saw the time. Eli had gone down to the buffet well over half an hour ago.

I guessed the restaurant could have been busy down there... But all Eli was doing was going down, grabbing some food from the buffet, and coming back up. We didn't know anyone else staying here, so it's not like she would have stopped to talk to a few people. And if someone had called her, like her father or Tess, she would have come back to the room to talk. Eli had lived in the supernatural community for too long to have potentially sensitive conversations out in the open, where anyone could eavesdrop.

So where was she?

Out of nowhere, my wrist burned as if I'd been stung by a wasp. On closer inspection, the pain was localized to the mark Eli had tattooed on me back when we were first together. I'd never felt any sort of sensation from it before, and for a moment I wondered if it was infected... Then I remembered how Eli described her foresight kicking into gear. She claimed it felt like a spark at the back of her skull, something she could feel but wasn't uncomfortable. The mark on my wrist was definitely trying to get my attention, as if this was my version of foresight.

And when I first felt the burning sensation under my mark, I was wondering where Eli was.

I sprinted out of the room toward the elevators and jammed the call button. When the carriage didn't get to my floor fast enough, I gave up on the elevator and headed for the stairs. I ran down to the lobby, taking the stairs two at a time, and flung open the doors. When I got to the front desk, what I saw was pure chaos.

The corridor between the lobby and restaurant had at least an inch of standing water in it, and more was pouring out of the ceiling. Hotel guests were standing on chairs and tables, demanding refunds and threatening to leave bad reviews, while the staff tried to herd them away from the mess. I ignored all of that, and continued my search for Eli. Someone wearing a name tag spotted me as I headed into the restaurant.

"Sir, we are requesting that all guests avoid the area until we get everything cleaned up," she said.

"Looks like you guys have some frozen, and now burst, pipes," I said.

She nodded. "This has never happened before."

"Seems to be happening a lot this winter. My wife came down earlier for the buffet," I said. "Mind if I peek inside to look for her?"

"There's no one in the restaurant except hotel staff," the hotel employee said. I looked past her, and saw she was right. Every table was empty, and no one was standing at the buffet.

"I must have been coming down while she was going up," I said. "Good luck with all of this."

I turned to go back up to our room, when I spied something on the ground near the main entrance. Lying in a pile of icy slush was a purple velvet hair tie.

When Eli walked out of our room, she'd had her hair up in the exact same tie.

I grabbed my phone and called Carmelo. He picked up on the first ring. "Baby brother."

"Moroz took Eli."

Chapter Twenty-Three
Frozen

I never thought I would actually freeze to death. Whine about being cold, yes. Turn up the thermostat so high Dan had heart palpitations about next month's heating bill, also yes. But to meet my demise due to being cold? That was just silly, a fate left to fictional characters like the matchstick girl and certain cartoon princesses.

Joke's on me, because my body is currently frozen. Frozen in ice, even.

When Moroz came up behind me and touched my shoulder at the hotel, he effectively froze my free will. He'd ordered me to leave the hotel with him, and my body followed him out to his car without question as my mind screamed for my legs to stop moving. As soon as I sat in the passenger seat of Moroz's car, he physically froze me, and ice started creeping across my skin. I was powerless to move or even ask him to turn the heater on. Now we were speeding out of the city and heading upstate, and there was an actual layer of ice on my skin, keeping my body immobile.

Oddly enough, even though ice completely covered my face, I could breathe just fine. My vision didn't appear compromised, either, but the ice was distorting things like an old, warped window pane. I wondered how long I could survive like this, frozen yet not dead. Not yet, anyway.

Eventually, the car stopped moving, and Moroz ordered me to get out. I obeyed, the icicles dangling from my hair and clothes falling off and breaking on the pavement as I followed him inside a store.

Not any store, I realized. His store. He'd brought me to Maple Acres.

"Get in the cooler," he ordered. I went to the large florist cooler at the back of the sales floor. All of the carefully bundled mistletoe bouquets hanging from the rafters were shriveled up, their leaves brown and crisp.

"When you took the mother plant, the children died soon afterward," Moroz said when he caught me looking at them. "Go to the back. Your new sister is already there."

I didn't question his latest order, and began heading toward the rear of the cooler. As soon as the door closed—meaning he was no longer in the same room as me—his control over my mind faded. That meant Dan was right, and Moroz needed to be in close proximity to influence someone or something. Maybe I could find a way to lock the cooler door from the inside, and either find an escape route, or dig in and wait for Dan to get here.

Because Dan was coming after me. I knew he would find me just as surely as I knew my own name. It was only a matter of time.

Now that Moroz's influence was fading, the already cracked ice that covered my skin and clothes was falling away from me. As I rubbed my arms, and searched for a thermostat to turn up or a tarp to throw over myself, I saw a woman lying in the corner between two sets of metal shelving. Her back was to me, but I recognized her long brown hair and cream sweater.

"Alicia," I said, as I knelt beside her and rolled her onto her back. Her lips were blue, and her skin was ice cold. "Alicia! Look at me!"

I pulled her onto my legs, sharing what was left of my body heat with her. The movement brought her back to reality, and her eyes fluttered open.

"That's it," I said, as I rubbed warmth back into her fingers. "Wake up for me. How long have you been here?"

"Eliza?" Alicia rubbed her eyes. "Why is it so cold?"

"We're in the plant cooler at Moroz's tree farm."

"That doesn't make any sense." Alicia sat up, and pushed back her hair. "How did we get here?"

"My guess is that he kidnapped you, same as me." I checked over Alicia's hands and face. She didn't seem to have any visible injuries, save for the chunks of ice stuck to her sweater and nestled in her hair. "What do you remember?"

"I was with Andreas," she began, then she smiled as her cheeks darkened. "You were right. He was happy to see me."

"I bet he was. Did you two go back to his place?"

"We did," she replied, as her face went crimson. "We talked, and... And it was just like we'd never been apart. After a while he said we should go to the diner and see his mother. They alternate the days they work around the holidays," she added.

"Have you ever met Andreas's parents before?" I asked. While it had nothing to do with our current circumstances, I was curious to know what Alicia thought about these legendary gods running a diner in Queens.

"Everyone knows Mama Anastasia," Alicia replied. "As for his father, I've met him a couple of times. He's very quiet, and imposing. Kinda scary, but the sort of scary that would protect you, if that makes sense."

"It does. Why were you two headed out to see Anastasia last night?" I asked, because when Dan and I were in the middle of a romantic evening, his parents were the last thing on my mind.

Alicia grabbed my hand. "Eli, Andreas asked me to marry him!"

I gasped, then I hugged her. "That's awesome! Did you say yes? Please tell me you said yes!"

"I did." She drew back, and I saw her grinning the biggest, happiest grin. "I said yes before he was even done asking."

"Then you guys were going out to share the good news," I said, and she nodded. "How were things at the diner?"

"We never got there. When we went out to the car, Mr. Moroz was standing in the garage. He said he was ready for me to go with him. I told him I thought about the job, and decided I didn't want it. Then he said it wasn't my choice, and that I reminded him of his daughter... Andreas pushed me behind him and they started shouting..." She shook her head again. "That's all I can remember. Do you think he hurt Andreas?"

"Maybe, but I don't think Moroz could hurt him too badly," I said. "Andreas is like Dan. They're both strong, and smart, and they'll come for us. Moroz is going to regret tangling with your family."

"Yeah he will," Alicia said, as she leaned against me. "Yeah, he will."

"Why did Moroz say I'm like his daughter?" Alicia asked. "I didn't even know he had a daughter."

I glanced down at Alicia. We were huddled in the far corner of the cooler with bags of pine bark mulch stacked against around us, trying our best to keep warm. A blanket or tarp would have been better, but we had to work with what we had.

"Her name was Natasha," I said. "Moroz accidentally killed her a while back."

"Great," Alicia said. "We're being held by a crazy man with actual daddy issues."

I smiled at the comparison, then my mind caught on something else Alicia said. "Moroz said that I'm like his daughter, too. You know, Dan and I suspected that Moroz has been targeting your family for a while, and I still think that's the case. However, I think we were wrong about why Moroz initially fixated on you guys."

"Really?" Alicia rearranged the mulch bags into something like an easy chair. "Tell me about it."

"Apparently, Moroz's daughter was all about taking care of him, until she found a boyfriend of her own. His name was Davos, and he was the son of Boreas." I took a breath, and decided to tell Alicia everything. "Boreas and Nonna were married. They still might be, but

I guess he moved on a while ago. You're all descended from the two of them."

"Was Boreas the husband after Enzo?"

"Right after, apparently. Anyway, we thought Moroz wanted to make Boreas's descendants suffer, but now he's said that you and I both remind him of his daughter. He also claimed that Natasha's mother was the strongest seer in Volgoda."

"Oh, she was powerful like Nonna?"

"You knew about Nonna being a seer?" I demanded.

"Of course," she said. "It's not like it's a secret."

I stared at Alicia. "Does everyone know about the magical side of things in Queens except Dan? Because he thought all of this was bunk before he met me."

"Don't blame Danny," Alicia said. "He had a lot on his plate growing up. Ma always leaned on him more than the older boys, and Danny's always acted like he was responsible for the world and everyone in it. I don't think he had time to think about magic."

"That sounds like Dan," I said. "A caretaker, even when he was a kid."

"You're a caretaker, too. You two are good together, really." Alicia laid her head on my shoulder. I wasn't sure if it was for warmth or camaraderie, but either reason was good with me. "I take it you're a seer, like Nonna?"

"I'm a seer on my dad's side. My mother is a witch."

"Oh, Mr. Moroz doesn't like witches. When we used to come up here as kids, he would tell us stories about evil witches, and how he would run them off his land." She was quiet for a moment. "So how can we use your witchyness against Moroz?"

"Not sure." I considered astral projecting to Dan, but he'd only ever projected once before. If I went to him while he was in his physical form, I didn't know if I would be able to get through to him. Then I thought about projecting to my dad or Tessa, but they were all the way in Massachusetts. Granted, phone calls were instantaneous and they could tell Dan where I was in seconds, but I wanted to reach out to someone closer to us.

Suddenly, I knew who to reach out to. Nonna.

"Alicia, I'm going to astral project to Nonna, and tell her where we are," I began, then I recalled my earlier concern about Moroz being able to sense astral forms. It was a rare talent, but one he might have.

"If Moroz comes in while I'm out, just tell him I'm asleep. Don't let on that I'm up to anything."

"I won't," she said. "Will you go to Andreas, too?"

"I have a feeling Dan's already with him."

Chapter Twenty-Four
She's Gone, Too

Less than twenty minutes after I called him, Carmelo pulled up in front of the hotel. He was driving my truck, which threw me for a second; in my panic over Eli's disappearance, I'd forgotten we'd traded keys the night before. I shook it off, and got into the passenger seat.

"You want us to sweep the hotel?" Carmelo asked. "It hasn't been long. He could have stashed Eli on site."

"She's not at the hotel," I snapped. "He took her, and I bet he took Alicia, too."

"Alicia? What makes you think that?"

"I can't raise her or Andreas," I replied. "I've called both of them at least ten times. And when I called Ma, she said Alicia never came home last night."

"All right." Carmelo radioed dispatch and told them he was investigating a possible missing person, then he pulled into traffic.

"Why possible?" I asked.

"Because if this is magic and shit like you say, I want to know what we're getting into. No reason to call in a task force that might make things worse," he replied. "Does Andreas still have that place off Ditmars?"

"Yeah. Eli and I were over there just yesterday." I unclenched my hand, and stared at Eli's purple hair tie resting against my palm.

Carmelo glanced over, saw me holding it. "That hers?"

"Yeah. I found it half frozen near the front desk. Same thing happened at the hotel that happened at Columbus Circle. The pipes froze and burst, made a huge mess. Moroz must have taken advantage of the confusion and grabbed her."

"Last night, I put a BOLO out on Moroz and his car," Carmelo said. "Might not do any good, but someone might see him." When all I did was nod, he added, "Hey. We're going to find her."

"I know. We will." A few strands of Eli's hair were still on the hair tie. I touched them, and swore to myself that I would find her, no matter what. "It's just that she's been kidnapped before."

"Really? By this guy?"

"No, no. It was in her hometown. It was her father's birthday, so she went out to get ingredients to make a cake. Two guys grabbed her and stuffed her in their trunk." I rubbed my eyes, trying to erase the image of a young, terrified Eliza being shoved into such a dark and cramped place. "She was only seventeen."

"Shit. No wonder it took her years to warm up to you. She must have been skittish as all hell after that."

"That's the thing. Eli's not skittish. She's strong, and smart, and tough as nails. Moroz better watch his back, because once she gets loose, she is going to destroy him."

Carmelo nodded. "Good girl. Is that what happened to her kidnappers? She get loose and teach them a lesson?"

"No. When her father found her, he got her out, then he burned the house down to the ground."

"Can't say I'd do it differently if it was my daughter. Her father go to jail?"

"Alex?" I scoffed. "Jail couldn't hold him."

"Good to know toughness runs in the family. We're here."

Carmelo parked in Andreas's driveway, and we went into the garage through the side door. We found Andreas sprawled across the concrete floor next to his Cadillac, his head bloody.

"I'll get an ambulance," Carmelo began.

"Hold on." I crouched next to Andreas and shook his shoulder. "Andreas, buddy."

Andreas's eyes snapped open. "Alicia! Where is she?"

"We think Moroz has her." I helped him to his feet while Carmelo did a sweep of the garage. "What happened?"

"We were on our way to the diner, to see my mother," he began. "Moroz was here, and he told Alicia she needed to go with him. She said no, then I told him to leave... and then it became cold. Everything went cold, and that's where my memory ends."

I nodded. "What time was this?"

"Just before ten last night," he replied.

"That means Moroz had Alicia for around nine hours before he grabbed Eli at the hotel this morning," Carmelo said.

Andreas stilled. "Moroz has both of them?"

"Yeah." I swallowed the lump in my throat, and focused on the garage ceiling. "She went down to the hotel restaurant to get us breakfast. That was around seven. She never came back up to our room."

"My guess is when Moroz couldn't get Eli last night at the Circle, he came straight here to snatch Alicia," Carmelo said. "Moroz couldn't get past your security," he pointed at the camera in the corner, "so he waited for you guys to come out. Then he stashed Alicia, and waited for an opportunity to grab Eli. He's probably holding them in the same location."

"We can't speculate," I said. "Them being held together is a best case scenario, but we need to consider all options."

"We need to know where Moroz is right now," Andreas said. "Once we find him, we can make him talk. Tell me where he is, and I'll bring hades to his doorstep."

My brother went still, and gave me a look. "Listen, I get that you're mad as hell, but I have to do things legally," Carmelo said.

"Then leave," Andreas said. "I'll find them on my own."

"Let's all take a breath," I said, then Carmelo's phone buzzed.

"Yeah," he barked into the receiver. "Uh, yeah. All right."

"Who is it?" I demanded.

"It's Ma. Nonna wants to talk to us, and this is a quote, about the girls." Carmelo held out his phone, and put it on speaker. "Go ahead, Nonna."

"Danny, you there?" came Nonna's voice.

"I'm here, Nonna," I said. "So is Andreas."

"Eliza and Alicia are at the tree farm," Nonna said.

"How do you know this?" Andreas asked.

"Because Eliza spirit come to me. Now Danny, you need to stop home and get my Acqua Tofana, and bring to farm."

"The poison?" I asked, as Carmelo's eyes bulged. "Did Eli ask for it?"

"No. Foresight tell me to send it with you."

Chapter Twenty-Five
Unmelting Ice

When I returned to my body after visiting Nonna, Alicia and I were no longer in the dark florist cooler. Instead, we were in a very bright office, and I was sitting behind a desk in a leather chair. At least it was warmer.

"What happened?" I asked, as I held up an arm to stave off the artificial light's assault on my eyeballs.

"A few minutes after you went under, Mr. Moroz came to check on us," Alicia said, as she wrung her hands. "He yelled your name and shook your shoulder, and wanted to know why you wouldn't wake up. I told him you were probably dying of hypothermia, so he threw you over his shoulder and had me follow him in here, and he dropped you in the chair. Then he locked us in here."

"How nice of him to look after us." I stretched the kinks out of my neck, then I started going through paperwork and ledgers scattered across the top of the desk.

"Did you see Nonna?" Alicia asked.

"I did," I replied. "I told her we were trapped here. She said she would have Patty call Carmelo, and he would send help. Why she's having Patty call him and not Dan, I have no idea."

"Carmelo's a captain in the force," Alicia replied. "What with Danny being a civilian now, Carmelo can try to keep him out of trouble." Alicia snorted. "As if that would ever work."

"Dan, in trouble? Surely you jest." Since there was nothing useful on top of the desk, I began opening drawers.

"What are you looking for?"

"Weapons," I replied; being that I'd only been running down to the hotel restaurant for breakfast, I hadn't armed myself the way I usually did. That had turned out to be a mistake. "Letter openers, pruning shears, mean looking pens. Anything pointy, really."

"If you're a witch and a seer, why do you need a weapon?"

"Being a seer isn't really an offensive power," I said. "I can sense spirits, and communicate with certain plants, but that's about it. As for my witch half, I only learned about that a few months ago. I know a few spells, but my magic backfires more often than not. However, poking someone in the eye with something sharp always works. Therefore, weapons."

"How are you new to being a witch? You said your mother is one. Didn't she teach you anything?"

"My mother left when I was eight." I looked up when Alicia gasped. "It's okay. I had my dad, and my grandmother. They were there for me, and taught me everything they knew about being a seer."

"Why did your mother leave? Did she go after someone magically?"

"No. She was just a jerk." Having finished going through the drawers, I spread my arsenal out on the desk. I'd found a metal stapler, a fountain pen, a handful of paper clips, and some push pins. "There has got to be something else we can use around here," I said, as I stood and approached the file cabinet.

"What kind of plants can you talk to?"

"Poisonous ones, usually," I replied. "My best friend calls them baneful herbs."

"Ooo, that sounds menacing!"

"It can be." The top drawer of the cabinet was full of nothing but files. Maybe I could give Moroz a particularly nasty paper cut. "If I have a relationship with a plant, like if it lives in my house or garden and I'm looking after it, I can usually communicate with it regardless of what kind it is. But I can always latch onto poisonous plants."

Alicia looked toward the door. I assumed the greenhouse was on the other side. "Isn't mistletoe poisonous?"

"Yeah, but it's a weak poison." The second drawer had tax records. I could always read them out loud and bore Moroz to death. "Besides, all the mistletoe in the cooler is dead."

"The stuff in the greenhouse looked good."

I stopped moving, my hands resting on another set of tax records. "What?"

"When he brought us out of the cooler, he took us through the greenhouse," Alicia said. "There were lots of plants. All of them looked green and healthy."

"Now you're talking." I went over to the door, which I really should have investigated before the desk or cabinet. Being frozen had knocked me off my game. I checked out the handle and learned that while it was locked, it was a simple indoor knob, and the upper half of the door was a window. I cupped my hands around my eyes and checked out the darkened area on the other side of the door. Just as Alicia said, it was the greenhouse. "Do me a favor, and straighten out some paperclips."

"What for?" Alicia asked, as she picked up a few clips.

"I'm going to pick the lock, then we're going to make friends with a few plants."

Picking the lock was easy. Getting into the greenhouse was also easy. When kidnappers made things easy, it was because they had laid a trap. Too bad for Moroz that this wasn't my first rodeo.

"Why are we going past the mistletoe?" Alicia asked, as we crept past the rows of cloned mistletoe and their host trees.

"They could be loyal to Moroz," I replied. "Also, they might be mad at me. I ran off with the mother plant."

"Eli!"

"Moroz was hurting it. I couldn't leave it behind." I glanced at the mistletoes, and hoped they understood. "Anyway, we need a stronger poison. What I wouldn't give for some belladonna or wolfsbane right now."

Beyond the mistletoes of questionable loyalty was a separate room in the greenhouse. We entered, and found long tables covered in holly specimens. As if that wasn't enough, mixed in were a few flats of lilies, Christmas cactuses, and laurels.

"All of this stuff is poisonous," I said, grinning like a mad scientist who had just harnessed lightning. "Alicia, all of these plants will work with us."

"What about this one?" she called from the far table. "I don't know what it is, but it looks magical?"

I went around the table, curious as to what a magical plant looked like. When I got to Alicia, I understood: she was staring at a much larger version of the little glass chamomiles that decorated all of Moroz's products. I got closer, and saw a tiny hammer and chisel on the far side of the glass plant, and a tray full of the smaller decorations.

"Why is Moroz chiseling out glass flowers?" I wondered, then I touched the main flower's petals.

They were ice cold, and even though these flowers were clear and shiny they were definitely not glass.

"When Dan and I talked to Boreas, he told us that Moroz's power comes from an unmelting piece of ice," I said.

"That sounds like a fairy tale," Alicia said. I gave her a look, then she motioned for me to continue.

"We thought Moroz kept the ice on him, but he keeps it here." I looked down into the planter, wondering what sort of soil an ice chamomile required, when I picked one up one of the smaller flowers.

"The decorations on Moroz's plants aren't glass, either," I said. "They're ice! It's how he's exerting his influence over such a vast distance!"

"Then we can stop him by melting the ice," Alicia said, then she frowned. "Only, this ice doesn't melt."

"No, it doesn't," I said, as I gazed at the table filled with poisonous plants. "But maybe melting it isn't our only option."

CHAPTER TWENTY-SIX
BROTHERS

"You can speed, you know," I said to my brother.

Carmelo glared at me, then he returned his attention to the road. "I am speeding."

"Speed more."

"Didn't I teach you how to drive? Keep your opinions under your hat."

"If we get a ticket, I'll pay it. You know I'm good for it."

"Oh yeah? You still owe me from that beach trip when you turned fourteen."

"That was a gift!"

"Enough, both of you," Andreas said from the back seat. "I understand you're both nervous, but Alicia and Eliza need us focused, and not squabbling like fools."

Carmelo looked like he was gearing up to give Andreas a piece of his mind, but I shook my head. While he concentrated on driving all of one mile over the speed limit, I turned around to talk with Andreas.

"You're pretty worried about Alicia," I said.

"Forgive me for speaking like that," Andreas said, as he stared at his hands. "I've had some experience with beings like Moroz. It never ends well."

"Experience, huh?" Carmelo asked, as he watched Andreas in the rearview mirror. "How does it end?"

"Badly." Andreas glanced up at me. "How are you so calm when that madman has both your sister and your wife?"

"I'm not calm," I replied. "I am absolutely freaking out, but if I waste all my energy worrying about things that might not even happen, I'll be a strung out mess by the time we get to the farm. Eli and Alicia need me at the top of my game."

"That's smart," Andreas said. "I wish I could me more like you, Dan. All I can think about is ripping Moroz's throat out."

"Can you do that?" I asked. "As in, have you inherited anything from your parents?"

"What, you think he can harness the cooking ability he inherited from Mama Anastasia and use that against Moroz?" Carmelo asked. He clearly was in the dark about Andreas's actual parentage.

"Mama would smack Moroz with a frying pan," I said instead of spilling the beans, then the two of us reminisced about the time she'd done just that to Frank Junior when she caught him stealing sweets. It was a gentle smack right on the ass, and it got the point across. Frank Junior never stole anything ever again.

"Last night, I was taking Alicia to see my mother," Andreas said quietly. Carmelo and I both shut up. "That's where we were going, when Moroz came. When Moroz took her."

"Yeah, you said you two were headed out to the diner," I said. "Were you two going out for dinner?"

"We probably would have eaten, yes, but that wasn't the main reason why we were going to the diner," Andreas replied. "I asked Alicia to marry me, and she said yes."

"That's great," I said. "Congratulations!"

"Welcome to the family," Carmelo said. "You do realize this means Danny and me get to torment you the way we torment Frank Junior and Joey?"

Andreas smiled. "We'll see about that."

"Guys," Carmelo said, as he turned into the tree farm's parking lot. "Brothers. We're here."

For the third time in a week, I was at Maple Acres. For a place that held such fond memories from when I was a kid, I'd really come to hate it here. Not bothering to hide our presence, Carmelo stopped the truck right in front of the shop's main door.

"When you get home, throw out all your mistletoe," I said to Carmelo, remembering how Ma had given him a bunch to decorate his place.

"What does fricken' mistletoe have to do with anything?" Carmelo demanded.

"All the stuff Ma gets is cloned from one of Moroz's demon plants," I replied, then I opened the glove box. "Where's my gun?" I asked, since it wasn't in its usual spot.

"In the back, with the rest." Carmelo opened his door, and tilted his head toward the back of the truck. "Come on. Check it out."

We got out and went to the rear door. Carmelo opened it, and revealed that he'd packed quite the arsenal. Even though there was a lot to choose from, I grabbed my usual sidearm while Carmelo went for the shotgun. My brother does not mess around.

"Andreas," Carmelo said, as we checked and loaded the guns. "You shoot?"

Andreas glanced inside the truck, then he focused on the storefront. "Thank you, but I do not care for guns."

"Okay, then." Carmelo slammed the rear door shut. "What's the plan? And he obviously knows we're here," he added, jerking his chin toward a surveillance camera perched on the corner of the store's roof.

"Let's move around back to the greenhouse," I said. "That's where Eli will be."

"Your girl really likes plants," Carmelo said.

"It's a family thing." Gun raised, I approached the building's corner and checked out the next leg of the path. All clear. "Her grandmother's house has this amazing solarium right off the kitchen. There's plants in there her family's been tending for generations."

"Keeping a garden is typical of seers," Andreas said. "They look after everything living, be they flesh and blood creatures or green and growing things. Their big hearts tend to be their downfall."

My gaze slid toward Andreas, but I didn't comment on his frank assessment of seers. Eli's compassion and empathy were two of the traits I loved most about her, and she had me to protect her big, beautiful heart. For now, I led us around the store on the same path my big-hearted wife and I had taken two days ago. When we rounded the corner, Moroz was standing in front of the greenhouse door.

"Danny, Carmelo," Moroz began. "How delightful to see you. Have you come by for more decorations?"

"My wife and my sister," I said, as I aimed my gun at his forehead. "Now."

Moroz bared his teeth. "Whatever has gotten into you? There's no one here but me."

"Moroz, I am placing you under arrest on suspicion of kidnapping," Carmelo said, as he raised his shotgun. "Get on your knees and put your hands on your head."

"I'll do no such thing," Moroz snapped. "This isn't the city. You have no jurisdiction here."

Carmelo showed Moroz his radio. "Ever hear of state troopers? On their way, as we speak. Are you gonna make this easy, or am I going to have to restrain you?"

A voice from above us yelled, "Hey!"

Bewildered, because I would know her voice anywhere and couldn't figure out why she was above me, I looked up and saw Eli standing on the store's roof. Behind her in the open window was Alicia.

"You two okay?" I asked, as Moroz screeched at them to get back inside.

"We're good," Eli replied. "Moroz stashed us in an office. I picked the lock, then we went exploring. I found this."

Eli held out what looked like a large glass flower, but I was betting that wasn't glass. When Moroz's face went white, then red, I knew that was his special ice, the piece Boreas had warned us about on the astral plane. It was the source of all his power, and the magic that had been screwing with my family since before I was born.

"Please, Eliza," Moroz began, then he gasped when Eli dangled the ice over the roof's edge.

"Don't you 'please, Eliza' me," she said. "You've caused enough pain, beginning with the murder of your daughter."

"And you can't replace her with us," Alicia yelled from the window. "She's gone, and Eli and me will never be her."

Out of the corner of my eye, I saw Andreas enter the store. Assuming he was going upstairs to get Alicia, and knowing Carmelo had his gun trained on Moroz, I focused on Eli. "Did he hurt you?"

"He froze me," Eli snapped. "Twice, this asshole froze me. And I hate being cold."

Eli raised her arm, and flung Moroz's ice flower down to the asphalt. As I watched it shatter against the blacktop, I remembered the bottle in my chest pocket. I pulled it out and poured Nonna's proprietary poison on top of the ice. The ice hissed and steamed, and started bubbling as it disintegrated into the ground.

"What have you done?" Moroz shrieked. The ice kept on melting. Up top, I saw Andreas in the window behind Alicia. Eli climbed back inside, then less than a minute later the three of them walked out of the place's front door. I clicked the safety on my gun, shoved it in the back of my waistband, and pulled my wife into my arms.

"Baby," I said, as I wrapped my arms around her and pressed my face against her hair. "You sure you're all right?"

"I'm okay." Eli tried to move back, but I wasn't done holding her. "Shouldn't we keep an eye on the bad guy?"

"Carmelo's got him." I tilted up her face, and said, "From now on, we get breakfast together."

"Together," she replied, then she tightened her arms around me. "I knew you would find me."

"Always, baby." I ran my hand over her hair, and picked out some wood chips. "Why is there mulch in your hair?"

"Alicia and I used it to keep warm." Eli moved so she could see Moroz, though she was still in my arms. I might never let go of her. "What did you pour on the ice?"

"Acqua Tofana."

"Nice. I'll make a seer out of you yet."

"Nonna suggested we bring it." Since Moroz was busy wailing over his melted ice, I turned to Alicia. She was wrapped up in Andreas much like Eli was wrapped up in me. "You okay, kid?"

"I'm better than okay," she said, as she smiled at Andreas.

"How do we punish him?" Andreas asked, jerking his head toward Moroz.

"We're doing exactly what I said," Carmelo replied. "I'm taking him in for kidnapping."

"I don't know if that's a good idea," I said, as visions of frozen prison pipes danced in my head.

"What do you mean, not a good idea?" Carmelo demanded, then his gaze focused on something behind me. "Grandpa Bo?"

Like a dream come to life, Boreas strode past us and halted in front of Moroz. He was wearing the same outfit of jeans and a flannel shirt that he had on the astral plane, though there was no doubt he was flesh and blood.

"You're pathetic," Boreas spat at Moroz. "A pathetic murderer. How dare you harm my family again, especially after what you did to Davos."

"I need a daughter," Moroz sobbed. "I must have a helper."

"What you need is to be held accountable for your crimes," Boreas said, then he faced us. "I can take Moroz where he won't hurt anyone ever again. Mistress, do you agree with this?"

It took Eli a moment to realize he was talking to her. "Yes," she replied. "The seer community has no grievance against Moroz. My complaints, which include his foul treatment of me and your family, are mine alone and do not represent the views of seers at large. I trust that you will see him judged accordingly."

Boreas nodded. "I shall, Mistress." He hauled Moroz up by the back of his neck. "Andreas, please give my regards to your parents. I've a feeling I'll be seeing your father sooner than later," he added, with a glare at Moroz.

"I shall, Boreas," Andreas said.

"Carmelo," Boreas continued, "Good work capturing Moroz. I am impressed by your ability to keep our family safe. And Daniel, my offer stands. If you need me, you have but to call."

"Thank you," I said. "For everything."

"Farewell." Boreas looked at each of us in turn, then he was gone.

"Good thing I never actually called the troopers," Carmelo said, as he rested the barrel of his shotgun against his shoulder. "This would require a hell of an explanation."

"You knew Boreas," Eli said. "You called him Grandpa Bo."

"I haven't seen him since I was a kid," Carmelo said. "I figured he'd passed, but I guess not."

"He's our grandfather?" Alicia asked. "Why does he look so young?"

"That, Alicia, is a very long story," I said, as I looked down and saw myself reflected in Eli's eyes, smiling like I was the happiest man in the world. At that moment, I was. "When we get home, ask Nonna. She'll tell you all about it."

Chapter Twenty-Seven
Piccolina

After Boreas took Moroz away, things at the farm immediately started changing, and not in a good way.

First, all of the plants died. They dramatically wilted en masse, and in less than five minutes, the greenhouse floor was carpeted in crunchy brown leaves. It was shocking, and made me wonder if all of the plants had been clones created through Moroz's magic as he'd done with the mistletoe, and thus couldn't survive without him. Normally I'd be sad at such a large loss of plant life, but if these plants had been kept alive artificially, I was glad they were now at rest.

Soon after the plants dried up to nothing, the wooden structures on the farm began deteriorating at a rapid rate. The paint chipped and flaked off, shingles cracked and fell to the ground, and the windows warped and shattered one after the other. By the time we drove out of the parking lot, Maple Acres looked more like a haunted house than a Christmas tree farm.

"So, you spoke to Boreas as the Mistress of Seers," Dan said, as we traveled back to the city. He was driving, which meant I got to sit in the front passenger seat. It also meant Carmelo was stuck in the back with Andreas and Alicia, which he was decidedly unhappy about. But it was Dan's truck, so Carmelo couldn't really complain.

"I did do that, didn't I." I'd been surprised when Boreas asked for my approval before he hauled Moroz off to what I could only assume was a supernatural jail cell. "Boreas was just being courteous. Someone as powerful as he is can do whatever he wants, regardless of how I feel about things."

"Or maybe he didn't want to risk angering the seers," Dan suggested. "I'm sure that wouldn't go over well, and face it, babe. Until the next generation comes along, the world will always see you as the leader of the seers."

"You're right." I'd been running from my calling as Mistress of Seers for almost half of my life, and for legitimate reasons. I didn't want to lead a magical community, or be the arbiter of their disputes and dole out punishments... but maybe I didn't have to do any of that. Maybe I could just be me, Eliza Moore Lyons, and the mighty Mistress of Seers at the same time.

Maybe, if I tried again, this time I could make it work.

"You know, I suppose leading the seers could be my calling," I said, just to find out how it sounded out loud. It wasn't too bad. "I mean, maybe someday. Not today."

Dan grabbed my hand, and kissed my knuckles. "If not today, maybe tomorrow, or next week, or next year. Whenever it happens, you know I'll support you."

I undid my seat belt and leaned across the center console so I could kiss his cheek. His whiskers had gotten even longer and softer, and I loved each and every one of them. "I know you will."

"No distracting the driver," Carmelo said from the back. "And buckle up, young lady."

"Yes, Officer Lyons," I said, as the rest snickered. Instead of following orders, I turned around and faced the lovebirds. "When are you two getting married?"

"Today?" Andreas asked, with a wide grin.

"We can't get married today," Alicia said. "It's Christmas Eve! There's going to be Nonna'a big lunch, then dinner, then we have to go to mass..."

"Tomorrow?" Andreas said, hopefully. "Actually, I have to run the diner tomorrow."

"That means I get pancakes?" I asked.

"Yes, Eliza," Andreas said. "I will make you pancakes whenever you want."

"They're not even that good," Dan grumbled, to which we all told him he was nuts. Andreas's pancakes were a legitimate treasure.

"But we'll get married soon," Alicia said, then she glanced up at Andreas. "Right?"

"Soon," he said, as he put his arm around her. "Whenever and where ever you want, a big ceremony or just the two of us. As long as I'm marrying you, it will be perfect."

"You should probably plan for big," Carmelo said. "After Danny and Eli here pulled their surprise wedding out of left field, Ma feels a little left out."

"That's not what happened and you know it," Dan said.

"Still, a ceremony with the whole family there would be nice," Alicia said; she was a peacemaker, just like Dan. "What do you say, Eli? Want to help me plan a wedding?"

"Sure, though I have to warn you. I've never planned a wedding. I didn't even plan my own."

"I've never planned one, either," Alicia said. "We can figure it all out together."

We started putting together Alicia and Andreas's wedding right there in the truck. By the time we reached Nonna's house, we had the bare bones of the ceremony sketched out. At first, both Andreas Alicia wanted a spring wedding, though, based on who Andreas's mother was, I suspected their reasons were different. However, waiting for spring meant waiting another few months, and that was something neither of them wanted to do. After a bit of debate, Carmelo ended up calling a friend of his who worked at city hall. The clerk's office was closed for the holiday, but it would reopen bright and early on December twenty-sixth.

"The office opens up at eight in the morning," Carmelo said, after he hung up. "You two can be married by eight thirty. Then we can all go back to the house for a party."

And that was exactly what happened.

After their small but perfect courthouse wedding, Andreas and Alicia Karras returned to Nonna's house, where the third family feast of the week was laid out. I'd never been surrounded by such joy. Even Enzo kept his wailing to a minimum.

Minutes before Patty and Nonna began serving lunch, there was a knock at the front door. Frank Senior opened it, and Andrea's parents joined us. Everyone already knew Mama Anastasia, and her husband was introduced as Hal, but I knew them for who they truly were: Persephone and Hades. Then again, they knew me, too.

"Daniel," Hal said, after he'd made his way toward Dan and me. "I haven't seen you since you and Andreas graduated high school. This lovely lady is your wife?"

"Yes sir, Mr. Karras. This is Eliza," Dan replied. "We got married last September."

After Hal offered us his congratulations, he said to me, "Your full name before marrying Daniel was Eliza Moore, was it not?"

If anyone ever asks you how it feels for the God of the Underworld to randomly know your surname, tell them it makes your skin crawl. "Yes, sir. My grandmother was Helena Moore, but I guess you knew that."

"I did, Mistress," Hal said. "My son speaks highly of you."

"Andreas is a good man," I replied. "Thank you for the help you offered us against Moroz. I won't forget it."

Hal dipped his chin. "Think nothing of it. We are now family, and family always answers the call for help."

I gazed at the packed family room, filled with Dan's extended family... and realized that they were my family, too. The seer community was large, and my grandmother had often hosted gatherings both big and small. Each and every one of those seers had my gran's back, just as

I knew they would have mine, but this was different. This was a sense of belonging I'd never experienced before.

I absolutely loved it.

"Piccolina," Nonna called from the downstairs kitchen.

When no one moved, Dan said, "Eli, she only calls you piccolina. You're up."

"Um, okay." I went downstairs and found Nonna standing in front of her stove. "Hey, Nonna."

"Hay for horse," Nonna said. "I make you something."

Nonna set a small glass bottle with a cork stopper on the counter. I gazed at it for a moment, then realized it could only be one thing. "You made me some Acqua Tofana?"

"I needed a new batch," she said, with a shrug. "Only family get to use. But you no get recipe!"

"Thank you, Nonna," I said. "I hope I never need to use it, but I know it won't ever fail me."

"Of course not," Nonna said, then her glamour slipped. For a moment she was a youthful appearing woman with dark hair piled on top of her head, and sparkling gray eyes.

"Is that how you look for Boreas?" I teased.

"It how I look all the time," she said. "I have to look like a nonna at home. Only you see me how I really am. Now help me carry up these cakes."

"Yes, ma'am."

We each lifted a tray of lemon and orange scented cakes and headed toward the stairs, then Nonna paused. "Danny choose well when he marry you," Nonna said. "I'm glad you here."

"Thank you, Nonna. I'm glad, too."

Nonna's cakes were a hit, not that I'd thought they wouldn't be. I had just grabbed my second slice of ricotta cake when Mama Anastasia approached me.

"Perhaps I should hire Esme," she said, as she helped herself to a slice of cake. "The diner doesn't have a dedicated pastry chef."

"Do you really make everything on site?" I asked. "Your kitchen must be huge."

"I'll let you in on a secret," Mama said, as she leaned closer. "The kitchen magically resets itself every night."

"I knew magic was involved!" Nothing tasted that good without a little magical help.

"The downstairs apartment in our townhouse also resets itself," Anastasia added, with a sly glance toward me. Just like that, visions of honey-stained sheets flashed behind my eyes. Nonna's light and fluffy cakes became a ball of lead in my stomach.

"I'm so sorry," I began, but Anastasia waved it away.

"Truly, think nothing of it," she said. "I do appreciate the effort you put in to clean up, but know that if you stay with us again, it's not necessary. Guests should enjoy themselves, and not feel like they are a burden in any way. Which you weren't," she added.

"Thank you." Even though Anastasia was being utterly gracious, my face warmed and my hands began trembling. I set down my plate, and asked, "So, does that apartment, um, influence people in any way?"

"You noticed," she said, with a grin. "When my husband and I were first together, our families did not approve. We made several such nests, where we could spend time alone and undisturbed. When we came to this country, we continued the tradition. Why, Andreas was conceived in that same apartment."

"Really." I looked across the room, and saw Andreas and Alicia sitting together on the couch. Even with the chaos of a dozen people around them laughing and telling stories, they were in their own world. "Will Andreas and Alicia live in the apartment now?"

"I believe so," Anastasia replied. "I can't wait to see what a year brings."

Hal beckoned Anastasia to his side, and she went to join her husband. I reclaimed my dessert plate, added another slice of cake, and went in search of my own husband. I found Dan on one of the upholstered easy chairs in the den, watching sports with his brothers. Since all of the chairs were occupied, I sat on his lap.

"Hey, baby," Dan said, as I made myself comfortable. "You enjoying yourself?"

"I am, and I brought cake." I fed him a forkful of cake, to his brothers' great amusement. "I was talking to Mama Anastasia. She said the apartment we stayed in is one of her and Hal's old love nests," I added, waggling my eyebrows.

"It sure was a love nest." He took the fork, and fed me a morsel of cake. "Speaking of which, when do you want to get out of here?"

"Up to you." Dan enjoyed being with his family, and I didn't want to rush him. "Do you think I should change my last name?"

"That's your choice," he said. "You could always hyphenate."

"She can't be Eliza Moore-Lyons," Carmelo the eavesdropper said. "That'll make her sound like a weird zookeeper."

We laughed, then Frank Junior asked, "Is it true you gave Danny that tattoo?"

"One hundred percent," I replied. "I used my dad's equipment."

"Think your father will give me a tattoo?" Frank Junior asked.

"That's a no," Joey interjected. "Your wife will kill you if you get a tat."

Carmelo chimed in, and soon the three of them were arguing about Frank Junior's potential future tattoo. While they were occupied, I snuggled closer to Dan, and said, "I just figured that since you keep calling me Mrs. Lyons, we might as well make it official."

"Yeah?" He tucked my hair behind my ear, his fingers lingering on my neck. "We can take care of that on Monday, then I can give you your present."

"Yours it at Gran's house," I said. "Dad and Tessa have custody of it until we get back."

"Custody? Please tell me it's not another demon."

"Don't worry, Mr. Lyons." I set our plate of cakes on the coffee table, and leaned my head on his shoulder. "You'll love it."

"Whatever you say, Mrs. Lyons."

CHAPTER TWENTY-EIGHT
FAMILY

Dan and I drove home to Massachusetts the next day, but not before we made several promises to come back to New York soon. Patty had decided that since Alicia would be moving in with Andreas, she would redecorate her room for Dan and me so we could stay there whenever we visited. While that was a nice gesture, I wasn't sold on sleeping down the hall from Dan's older sisters, and the wailing spirit of Nonna's first husband. Hotels would do me just fine.

After we dropped off our suitcases at the house, and brought in our mail, Dan and I headed to Gran's so we could visit my dad and Tessa. When we were halfway there, I sent Tess a warning text.

Eli: Five minute warning

Eli: Is he okay? Are the cats mad?

Tessa: He's adorable and snuggly. The cats are indifferent, which is probably a best case scenario. I just fed him, so he's in a good mood.

"What are you and Tess talking about?" Dan asked.

"Your present."

"Eli! I left yours at the house!"

"It's okay. You can give it to me later."

Dan pestered me for hints about his present, but I didn't give in. Then we pulled onto Gran's gravel driveway, and my excitement got the better of me as I practically leapt out of the truck and burst into the mudroom. The Feline Federation was lined up and waiting for me, and they did not look pleased.

I needed to issue my apology now.

"Look, it was only temporary," I said to their leader, Pumpkin. "He's coming home with us. Promise."

"Who's coming home with us?" Dan asked. I stepped aside, and gestured for him to enter the kitchen. He did, saw my father standing at the counter.

"Hello, Dan," my dad said, then he leaned toward the door to the living room. "Isa, they're here!"

"Hey, Alex," Dan said. "Eli said someone's coming home with us?"

"That's correct," Dad, said, then Tessa entered the kitchen. In her arms was a small, fluffy brown puppy.

"Hey, look at this guy," Dan said. "You guys got a dog?"

"No, silly," I said, as Tessa handed the puppy to Dan. "You got a dog. He's your Christmas present, and he's been staying with Dad and Tess while we were in New York."

Dan stared at the puppy in his arms, then he looked at me. "You got me a dog?"

"Didn't you want one?" I asked, suddenly panicked that my perfect gift wasn't so perfect.

"I did," Dan said, to my relief. "What's his name?"

"He doesn't have one yet," my father said. "However, he does come with about a ton of toys and other supplies."

"We may have spoiled him," Tessa added.

"That's cool." Dan lifted up the puppy so they were eye to eye. "He's a good boy, deserves to be spoiled." He held the pup against his shoulder with one arm, and extended the other to me. "Thank you, baby," Dan said, as he wrapped his arm around me. "He's the best gift I've ever gotten."

Dan named the puppy Stuart, and the five of us spent the evening together having a quiet post-Christmas dinner. When I told my father that I was considering becoming a low-key version of the Mistress of Seers, he told me he'd had similar ideas about his own place in the community.

"As the marksman, I've been traveling the world for decades," he began, "but things aren't like they were in the old days. What with cell phones and the internet, people can contact me in seconds. I don't need to spend my time journeying from one clan to the next on the off chance that they might need me. If they need me, they can call me, or they can come here."

"I thought you loved traveling."

"I do, but I think it's time for me to stay in one place for a while." He glanced toward the far side of the room, where Tessa and Dan were teaching Stuart to give them his paw. The little guy was a fast learner. "For now, I'd like to stay home, with our family."

I leaned against his arm. "I like that. My first official of act as Mistress of Seers is to declare that the marksman is to remain at his home base for at least one year."

Dad looped his arm around my shoulders. "You will be a wonderful Mistress. I'm certain of it."

Later on, Dan and I took Stuart home and got him set up with his dog bed in the kitchen, then we went upstairs. Dan led me to his side of the walk-in closet, and pulled a blue velvet box out of his dresser.

"As you know, I never got to pick out a ring for you," he began, as he handed me the box. "I decided it's time to make up for it."

I opened the box and gasped. Dan had gotten me a necklace and earring set. The pendant was a teardrop shaped moonstone, and the silver chain was dotted with tiny deep blue sapphires. The earrings each featured a dangling moonstone drop and were topped with a single sapphire.

"They're beautiful," I said, as I touched the pendant. "Why moonstones?"

"They reminded me of you. Hold up your hair." I did, and as I stood in front of the mirror, Dan put the necklace on me. "Beautiful," he said, after he'd fastened the clasp. "Just like you."

New Year's Eve came and went, and we took New Year's Day off to sleep in and relax as much as we could. Stuart had other ideas, but it was okay. Even though he was an excitable puppy, just like Dan said, he was a good boy. We went down to city hall the following day, and I filled out the paperwork to officially become Eliza Lyons, and apply for a dog license. Dan, Stuart, and I were now a family of three.

The next day was back to work at Nine Lives Investigations. Dan and I accepted and closed a record number of cases that month, so many that we took out a special account for the extra funds we'd earned. We didn't have a lot of expenses—our house was paid for, as were both of our cars—and Dan thought investing the money was smart. And who knew, if these investments worked out, maybe we wouldn't have to work forever.

As for me resuming my position of Mistress of Seers, no one had come asking for my help. Yet.

Our streak of closed cases hit a speed bump in early February. I caught some sort of bug, and its main symptom was fatigue. I'd never been so tired in my life, not even during the year I'd decided to train for a half marathon. Dan diagnosed me as overworked, and we cleared our schedules for the last week of the month. It was nice to sleep late for a few days, even if Stuart stuck his cold dog nose on me at the crack of dawn anyway, but on the third day of enforced rest I remained as exhausted as ever.

"You sure you shouldn't see a doctor?" Dan asked, as he made breakfast. While he scrambled eggs, I sat at the table, willing more coffee to appear in my cup. Sadly, it wasn't working.

"I don't know what a doctor could really do for me," I replied, leaving off how I despised doctors. That, Dan already knew. "I don't have any symptoms, other than being tired."

"Maybe it's Seasonal Affective Disorder, and you'll be better once the days get a bit longer," he suggested.

"Hopefully," I said, around a yawn. "I'd like to have my energy back."

Dan's phone beeped. He moved the pan off the burner, and went to check it. Since my coffee cup remained maddeningly empty, I dragged myself out of my chair and toward the coffeemaker.

"Who is it?" I asked as I poured. "Is it a new client?"

"Not hardly," he said, as he grinned. "Get this. Alicia's pregnant!"

"Really! That was fast!" Mug refilled, I turned toward the stove, and almost gagged when I saw the fluffy yellow eggs sitting in the frying pan. "I'm going to have cereal."

"Alicia says she's around six or eight weeks along, which means it happened right around Christmas," Dan continued.

"She's giving you all the gritty details?" I poured Grape Nuts into a bowl, looked at the jug of milk in the fridge and decided against adding some to my cereal, then I grabbed a spoon and started eating.

"Always has. I'm a better listener than Theresa or Dolores."

I snorted, but kept my opinions of those two to myself. "Isn't six weeks awful early? How can she even know already?"

"Funny you should ask," Dan said. "She says she had unusual fatigue, and suddenly didn't like certain foods that she'd always eaten with no problem. When she mentioned these symptoms to Andreas's mother, Anastasia suggested a pregnancy test."

"I guess smashing Moroz's ice really did break that geas on your family," I said, as I spooned up my dry cereal. "She didn't have to wait for you to have a kid before she could get on the parenting train."

"Guess not." Dan looked up at me, and frowned. "Babe, why are you having cereal without milk?"

"The milk is gross, just like the eggs."

Dan looked pointedly at the eggs. "You love eggs."

"Not today I don't." I drank some coffee to wash down my dry as dust cereal. When I lowered my mug, Dan was wearing the most perplexed face I'd ever seen. "What?"

"You've got fatigue, and you're not eating the way you usually do," he said.

"What? No. No, no, no. I am not—"

My thoughts whirled as my throat burned, then I spun around and retched into the sink. I turned on the faucet, and rinsed out my mouth with a handful of water. By the time I shut off the water, Dan was standing next to me with a kitchen towel in his hands.

"Get off your feet," he said, as he guided me back to my chair. I wiped my mouth, then I made the mistake of looking toward the stove. When I caught sight of the eggs, my stomach roiled again.

"I'm fine," I said. "I just have the flu or something."

"Eliza," Dan said. "Are you sure that's what's happening?"

I looked from Dan's concerned face, to the eggs I couldn't fathom eating, to my milkless cereal. It couldn't be true, and yet...

"Shit."

I hope you enjoyed Eli and Dan's latest, chilliest adventure. Book 6, Mandrake, is available here: https://books2read.com/poisongarden -mandrake. Turn the page for a sneak peek!

Chapter Twenty-Nine
Mandrake

We still weren't talking about it.

After Dan got the text announcing Alicia's pregnancy, and I threw up at the sight of a pan full of scrambled eggs, I went back to bed. Maybe this was all a dream. Or maybe it was reality, and I could get a do over. Not that I could, or even would, change things. I just needed time to catch my breath, and think.

Dan let me wallow in my feelings for about an hour before he came to check on me. He sent Stuart in first, and let the pup gallop around the room for a few minutes before he joined us. Stuart *wuffed* at the sight of him, so Dan picked him up and plopped him on the bed.

"Hey, Stuart." I scratched behind his ears, always up and at attention, although the left one tended to flop over. "You keeping an eye on Dan?"

"He supervised as I cleaned up from breakfast, then he let me take him out," Dan said; soon after we brought him home, it became apparent that Stuart now ruled the house. We were all okay with that. "How are you feeling?"

"Better," I said, though I was still tired. However, the lack of eggs in close proximity to me meant I was no longer nauseous, and that was a definite improvement. "Sorry I got all dramatic earlier."

"It's all right. We just won't have eggs for a while." Dan sat next to me. I snuggled up against him, then Stuart decided to get in on the action and wedged himself between us. "Want to talk about it?"

"I... I just want to stay like this, for now."

Dan kissed my hair. "Sounds like a plan."

And so we sat, silently holding each other while the biggest elephant in the history of elephants sat in the room with us. After a few minutes of forced relaxation, my phone beeped.

"You gonna get that?" Dan asked, then his beeped. "Might be a case."

"Might be." I grabbed my phone, and saw a text from Jill Sanders. She was one of Dan's closest friends from when he was on the police force. "Jill texted me."

"Me, too. She said there's something, and I quote, weird happening downtown."

"That's what she said to me, too," I said, then I replied.

Eli: How weird, and where downtown?
Jill: Very, and at the park next to City Hall.
Eli: We'll be there in ten.

"You sure you're up for it?" Dan asked. "I can go alone."

"I'll be fine," I replied, as I got out of bed and went in search of my boots. "Besides, if this is magical weirdness you'll need me."

"All right, babe," Dan said, then he shooed Stuart off the bed and grabbed his coat. "Let's check out the latest nonsense."

Fifteen minutes later, Dan parked on Main Street. We saw the police cars congregated around the park entrance, then I saw something more interesting than a few cruisers with flashing lights. Even though it was still winter, there was a cluster of mandrake plants at the base of the lamp post.

"Here's the first something weird." I crouched down, and poked at the rosette of leaves. "I've never seen mandrakes in this park."

"And that's something you would have noticed?" Dan asked.

"Oh, yeah. As far as magical plants go, mandrake is herbal royalty." I straightened up, and saw another one of the plants farther inside the park. "There's more."

"Let's follow the trail," Dan said. "Gotta say, I'm almost used to plants asking you for help."

"Almost?"

"I'm holding a grudge against the mistletoe."

I grabbed Dan's hand, and we followed the mandrakes. They were scattered around the park, poking up through the snow and hiding behind benches and statues. The path wended behind City Hall, close to where the police had set up. While Dan looked for Jill, I visually tracked the mandrakes to the base of an oak tree, then I remembered a certain fact about these plants.

Mandrakes were said to sprout beneath a hanged man.

I looked up, and saw three bodies swaying from the upper branches. Pinned to the center body's torso was a sign that had "witch" scrawled across it in violent red letters.

"There you are," Jill said, as she and Dan joined me. "Like I was telling Dan, someone staged the execution of three supposed witches behind City Hall."

I looked from the Jill, then back up at the bodies, and puked.

"You okay?" Jill asked.

"No." I wiped my mouth, and looked up at the bodies. *Witch* bodies. If people were out here murdering witches, how could I bring a baby witch into the world? "I'm pretty far from fine."

Get your copy of mandrake here: https://books2read.com/poisongarden-mandrake

Also By Jennifer Allis Provost

The Chronicles of Parthalan, a six volume epic fantasy (and one short story collection)
Heir to the Sun
The Virgin Queen
Rise of the Deva'shi
Pieces of Parthalan: Six All-New Stories From The Land Of Parthalan
Golem
Elfsong
Sunfall

The Copper Legacy, a four book urban fantasy:
Copper Girl
Copper Ravens
Copper Veins
Copper Princess
A duology based in the Copper world:
Redemption
Salvation
Poison Garden, an urban fantasy filled with seers, witches, and one seriously hot detective:
Belladonna
Oleander
Bleeding Hearts
Thornapple
Wolfsbane
Mistletoe
Mandrake

**Gallowglass, an urban fantasy set in
Scotland and New York:**
Gallowglass
Walker
Homecoming
The Shades of Elphame
**Winter's Queen, an urban fantasy set in
Scotland and Elphame:**
Touch of Frost
Giant's Daughter
Elphame's Queen
**Merrowkin, an urban fantasy set in Ireland
above and below**
Merrowkin
Death's Door
Manannán's Pearl
Changes, a contemporary romance:
Changing Teams
Changing Scenes
Changing Fate
Changing Dates

About the Author

Jennifer Allis Provost is a native New Englander who lives in a sprawling colonial along with her beautiful and precocious twins, a dog that thinks she's a kangaroo, a parrot, a junkyard cat, and a wonderful husband who never forgets to buy ice cream. As a child, she read anything and everything she could get her hands on, including a set of encyclopedias, but fantasy was always her favorite. She spends her days drinking vast amounts of coffee, arguing with her computer, and avoiding any and all domestic behavior.

Find Jenn on the web here: http://authorjenniferallisprovost.com/

For up to the minute sale notifications, follow her on Bookbub here: https://www.bookbub.com/profile/jennifer-allis-provost
   For exclusive content, follow her on Patreon: https://www.patreon.com/jenniferallisprovost/
   Friend her on Facebook: http://www.facebook.com/jennallis
   Follow her on Instagram: @jenniferaprovost
   Happy reading!

www.ingramcontent.com/pod-product-compliance
Lightning Source LLC
Chambersburg PA
CBHW021551310726

48972CB00003B/777